AND TO ALL
A GOOD BITE

ALSO BY DAVID ROSENFELT

ANDY CARPENTER NOVELS

Dogged Pursuit
The More the Terrier
Dog Day Afternoon
'Twas the Bite Before Christmas
Flop Dead Gorgeous
Santa's Little Yelpers
Holy Chow
Best in Snow
Dog Eat Dog
Silent Bite
Muzzled
Dachshund Through the Snow
Bark of Night
Deck the Hounds
Rescued
Collared
The Twelve Dogs of Christmas
Outfoxed
Who Let the Dog Out?
Hounded
Unleashed
Leader of the Pack
One Dog Night
Dog Tags
New Tricks
Play Dead
Dead Center

Sudden Death
Bury the Lead
First Degree
Open and Shut

K TEAM NOVELS

Good Dog, Bad Cop
Citizen K-9
Animal Instinct
The K Team

THRILLERS

Black and Blue
Fade to Black
Blackout
Without Warning
Airtight
Heart of a Killer
On Borrowed Time
Down to the Wire
Don't Tell a Soul

NONFICTION

Lessons from Tara: Life Advice from the World's Most Brilliant Dog

Dogtripping: 25 Rescues, 11 Volunteers, and 3 RVs on Our Canine Cross-Country Adventure

AND TO ALL A GOOD BITE

David Rosenfelt

MINOTAUR BOOKS
NEW YORK

This is a work of fiction. All of the characters, organizations, and events portrayed in this novel are either products of the author's imagination or are used fictitiously.

First published in the United States by Minotaur Books, an imprint of St. Martin's Publishing Group

EU Representative: Macmillan Publishers Ireland Ltd, 1st Floor, The Liffey Trust Centre, 117–126 Sheriff Street Upper, Dublin 1, DO1 YC43

AND TO ALL A GOOD BITE. Copyright © 2025 by Tara Productions, Inc. All rights reserved. Printed in the United States of America. For information, address St. Martin's Publishing Group, 120 Broadway, New York, NY 10271.

www.minotaurbooks.com

Library of Congress Cataloging-in-Publication Data

Names: Rosenfelt, David, author
Title: And to all a good bite / David Rosenfelt.
Description: First edition. | New York : Minotaur Books, 2025. | Series: An Andy Carpenter novel ; 32
Identifiers: LCCN 2025018526 | ISBN 9781250324573 (hardcover) | ISBN 9781250324580 (ebook)
Subjects: LCGFT: Fiction | Detective and mystery fiction | Novels
Classification: LCC PS3618.O838 A826 2025 | DDC 813/.6—dc23/eng/20250520
LC record available at https://lccn.loc.gov/2025018526

The publisher of this book does not authorize the use or reproduction of any part of this book in any manner for the purpose of training artificial intelligence technologies or systems. The publisher of this book expressly reserves this book from the Text and Data Mining exception in accordance with Article 4(3) of the European Union Digital Single Market Directive 2019/790.

Our books may be purchased in bulk for specialty retail/wholesale, literacy, corporate/premium, educational, and subscription box use. Please contact MacmillanSpecialMarkets@macmillan.com.

First Edition: 2025

10 9 8 7 6 5 4 3 2 1

AND TO ALL A GOOD BITE

Jeff Wheeler had never been much of a fan of the holiday season.

He wasn't the "bah, humbug" type . . . far from it. But his attitude about it came from a more practical reason. It was too damn cold. Jeff was into tennis, and golf, and swimming, none of which one can do in snow boots.

Additionally, Jeff owned a small construction company that mostly built and renovated houses, which meant he and his employees were outside a great deal. So the holiday time of year, leading to the long winter that followed it, made their jobs more difficult and far less comfortable.

But this year was going to be different. He had just finished a large job, a house in Teaneck, and could afford to take a break for a while. And he was sure as hell going to take advantage of that respite.

He was planning to take his girlfriend, Lisa Dozier, to an island called Virgin Gorda, in the British Virgin Islands. It was said to be as beautiful and romantic a place as existed, the perfect location for him to propose marriage. Which is exactly what he was going to do.

And the whole thing was going to be a total surprise . . . sort of.

He would tell her about the trip that night, though of course without mentioning the proposal. He had no doubt her answer would be yes, both to the trip and the marriage. They had both understood for a while that they would wind up together. So it would not come as a shock to her, but more of a very pleasant surprise.

It made it even tougher to keep the secret because he literally had the ring in his pocket as he went to pick her up from work that night. He had just gotten it from the jeweler and hadn't had a chance to go home and leave it there. It would take all his willpower not to give it to her right away, but he would resist the temptation.

Lisa worked in finance for a large firm with a home office in Paramus, just off Route 17. She had gotten her MBA at the University of Delaware and worked in two other places before getting her current job at Marstan Industries.

What she did daily sounded a little boring to Jeff, but there was nothing boring about Lisa once she left the office. She was upbeat and always ready for anything fun. In Jeff's mind, everything about her was special, and he'd known it the moment he met her.

Jeff parked in the lot behind the Marstan building; it was almost 8:00 P.M. and only a handful of cars were there. It was only a few seconds after he got out of his car that the invisible wave hit him. He didn't know what it was, which made it disorienting in the extreme. But it actually felt like it was compressing his skin, and it knocked him back against the car.

For a brief moment he thought he might have been

hit by lightning, but that couldn't be it, since he was still conscious and alive. He looked around to see if anyone else had felt the incredible jolt, but he was alone in the parking lot.

He smelled the smoke before he saw it. When he looked at the building, it was pouring from a window that appeared to have been blown out, and then some was coming from the roof. And then he saw the flames, flicking through the blown-out windows on the third and fourth floors.

Lisa's office was on the fourth floor.

Jeff ran to the back door of the building and found it open. It led into the lobby, which was starting to fill with a choking smoke. Having visited Lisa here before, he knew where he was going, and he ran toward the stairs.

He went up three steps and saw a wall of flame and smoke above him. There was simply no going through it.

In a panic, he looked for another way up, but didn't remember any and doubted there was one. There was simply no way to get up there.

And then he heard it. It was a strange sound, almost a whimper, and he ran toward it. In the thick smoke he stumbled on it before he even saw it.

It was an open-air crate and there was a dog in it. He grabbed at the latch, which was already getting hot. He opened it, grabbed the dog, and ran back toward the door to the parking lot, carrying the dog and fighting to breathe the whole way.

He made it. He put the dog in the back of his car and ran around to the front of the building to see if there was an alternative way in, which might lead to another way up those steps.

There was not another way, and he was helpless.

He had saved the dog.

But he had not saved Lisa.

The main room at Echelon, a prestigious auction house on Madison Avenue in New York City, was filled to capacity.

But there was not going to be an auction that day; instead there would be a press conference. It had been scheduled a week in advance, with the tease that they would be making a major announcement in the art world.

Considering that Echelon was known throughout the fine-art community to be staid and conservative, the event was eagerly anticipated and speculation was rampant. Every art journalist and critic in New York was there, in addition to many from out-of-state outlets.

This was going to be big.

The conference was called for 1:00 P.M., but it wasn't until almost 1:20 that two men strode into the room and up to the stage where the auctioneer would normally stand. Both men were immediately recognizable to those in attendance.

One was Wallace Linder, the managing director of Echelon for the last twenty-two years. Linder was universally respected and admired and had guided Echelon to its position alongside Sotheby's and Christie's at the top of the industry.

The other man was Stanley Franklin, a wealthy businessman and private art collector. Franklin was well-known in the community as well, not only for his own collection and fine taste, but for his ability to attract some of the finest works from people looking to sell.

Linder spoke first. "Ladies and gentlemen, this is an exciting day for Echelon and for the art community that we live in and love. I believe most if not all of you know Stanley Franklin, and I am going to turn this over to him to make the announcement. I'll come back afterwards and we will both take any questions you may have. Stanley?"

Franklin moved to the microphone. "Thank you, Wallace. As I am sure you know, before and during World War Two, the Nazis stole and hid many of the finest works of art the world has ever known. Many of them have never been recovered, and the mysteries of their disappearances have remained unsolved for eighty years.

"I will admit to being obsessed with this, and many of you know that I have spent very considerable time and money in search of these lost treasures. I have hired investigators who have spent countless weeks and months, sometimes years, in Europe and South America, following up on every lead and tip and piece of information we could find.

"It has been a wild ride, with positive leads and apparent momentum, and then crushing disappointments, only to be followed by renewed optimism. And so on and so on.

"But I am here today to say that our efforts have now

been successful beyond our wildest dreams. We uncovered a secret, climate-controlled room in an underground bunker in Poland that held fourteen works of true masters. We are talking about such geniuses as Vermeer, Dalí, Picasso, Gauguin, Monet, and others.

"The works are at a location which for the moment will remain undisclosed, but authentication, including radioactive carbon dating, has been completed. Ladies and gentlemen, these are the real deal . . . and easily the most exciting personal event of my lifetime. Wallace?"

Linder rejoined Franklin on the podium to take questions. But first Linder said, "The collection, in its entirety, will be sold at auction, with the date still to be determined. Individual pieces will not be up for bid; it will be available only as a collection. When all the details and photographs of the works are revealed, we expect extraordinarily healthy interest. Now we will take your questions."

Linder called on a journalist, who asked if it was known what the minimum bid would be.

"Yes, one hundred and fifty million dollars." Linder smiled. "We view that as a starting point."

The next question was to Franklin. "Will details of how this find was accomplished be forthcoming?"

"Within limits. There are some confidentiality agreements that have been signed with informants. Even to this day, some of this is politically sensitive and even potentially dangerous. But we will try to be as forthcoming as possible."

A follow-up question to Franklin was "You referred to

spending considerable money on this quest. Care to say how much?"

Franklin smiled. "I do not care to say. Sorry."

"How about a ballpark figure?"

Another Franklin smile. "Let's just say it was in eight figures, but no matter how many times you ask, I'm not going to tell you what those figures were."

"What about the original owners of these paintings? Should the works not be returned to their estates?"

Franklin nodded. "Excellent question. Every effort has been made to locate anyone with a claim to these works. Two have been made, and if they are verified, those paintings will revert to the claimants. But most are unknown; the descendants of the original owners may not have ever known about them. In some cases, the works themselves were not known to have existed.

"But we have been painstakingly going through this research and tracing process, which is why it has been delayed until now."

The same journalist who asked about the original owners was called on again and asked, "Can you talk more about how the authentication was done?"

Linder nodded. "Certainly. Both Mr. Franklin's experts and our experts here at Echelon have examined the paintings and run tests on them. All passed with flying colors. But to be extra-sure, we secretly coordinated with the Metropolitan Museum of Art. They were nice enough to assist us, and their people performed radioactive carbon dating on two of the canvases.

"You can contact them for more information, but their

work confirmed the authenticity of these pieces. And when you see the beauty of them, you will have no doubt.

"There is more to come, ladies and gentlemen," Linder added. "But as you might imagine, we are terribly excited. It is certainly the greatest discovery of this kind in my lifetime. Thank you all for coming."

Franklin held up a hand and said, "One moment, please. I want to say something else. This is an incredibly emotional day for me, as it is the one-year anniversary of the horrible gas-leak explosion at my company, which took the lives of seven wonderful people. As you know, a significant amount of artwork was destroyed that day as well.

"I would just like us to take a brief moment of silence to remember those seven people. May they rest in peace."

The room went silent for a moment and then Franklin said, "Thank you for that. And thank you for coming."

As a football fan, I don't ask for much.

All I really want is for the Giants to be competitive; I want games late in the season to matter. I don't even necessarily care if they make the playoffs; I would just like them to be in contention for a while.

I dream of a Thanksgiving weekend during which the Giants play a meaningful game, when their record has not already eliminated them. I'm told it used to happen with some regularity. The story has been passed down through the generations, probably dating back to one of my great-ancestors . . . maybe someone named Nehemiah or Josiah Carpenter.

Alas, those mythical glory days are gone. I, Andy Carpenter, have mostly known New York Giants football misery, albeit with a couple of great Eli Manning–led exceptions. Yet I still dream. . . .

Otherwise, Thanksgiving is my favorite holiday. Great food, no work, and wall-to-wall football, college and pro. Of course, I'm mostly retired from my defense-attorney career, so the "no work" part is pretty much the same as on the nonholiday weekends.

The only negative that I can think of is the incessant

Christmas music that my wife, Laurie Collins, force-feeds throughout the house on our stereo system. She thinks that Christmas runs from Halloween until Presidents' Day in February, which makes us the only house in Paterson that hums for four months to the music of Bing Crosby.

I'm sure he was popular in his day, but if I were an accused suspect, being forced to listen to hour after hour of ol' Bing hoping for snow would get me to confess, whether I was guilty or not.

I guess it could be worse; there could be Thanksgiving music playing, if any exists. I live in fear that Laurie will find a *Greatest Hits of the Pilgrims* album. Who knows? Maybe there used to be a genre of music called Plymouth Rock.

Tomorrow is Thanksgiving, which is why Laurie has spent most of the day in the kitchen. Our sixteen-year-old son, Ricky, is at a friend's house, since school is off this week. I have been spending the day mostly napping and gearing myself up for the rigorous football-watching weekend to follow. When awake, I am usually doing remote-control hand exercises. Fortunately, I can work the remote efficiently with either hand.

The phone rings and Laurie yells out, "Andy, can you get that?"

This may not seem like a big deal to normal human beings, but to me it represents something of a problem. I hate talking on the phone; it is not natural conversation. There is never room for pauses as there is if you're in a room with somebody. The whole purpose of being on the phone is to talk, so if no one is talking, even briefly, it's unnatural.

The worst is when people call without a specific purpose other than to say hello and chat. I keep waiting for them to get to the point, when in fact there is no point. I'm constantly looking for an opportunity to say, "Well, okay then, thanks for calling." Such opportunities are often far too rare.

Caller ID is one of the greatest inventions of all time, ranking up there with electricity, the automobile, and the point spread. I cannot tell you how many torturous phone calls it has helped me avoid.

This time, however, it's not that helpful. It says CAROL HENDRI, and I assume the last name has been trimmed for space. Maybe Hendrickson?

That doesn't matter because I don't know anyone named Carol. Maybe Laurie does, but that possibility is not enough to get me to answer the call. Instead I'll let the machine do the honors and pick up if an incoming message warrants it. Few messages scale that mountain.

The message comes on and it's a clearly distraught woman's voice. "Mr. Carpenter, this is Carol Hendrickson, Jeff's sister. Jeff is in trouble; if you're there, please pick up."

I don't know what to do. Not only don't I know this person, I also don't think I know anyone named Jeff. So she must have a wrong number, even though she is looking for "Mr. Carpenter." Maybe she is trying to reach a different Mr. Carpenter and was given this number by the information operator.

Are there still information operators?

I don't want to pick up, but I have to. She just sounds so desperate that not to do so would be awful. And in the likely event that she's trying to reach a different Carpenter, I can set her straight so she can correct her mistake.

"Hello? This is Andy Carpenter. I—"

"Thank God you're there."

That's a bad sign; the use of the name Andy did not dissuade her or make her realize the errors of her ways. "Who is this?" I ask, though I'm pretty sure the answer will be "Carol Hendri . . ." something.

"Carol Hendrickson. We met about a year ago. I'm Jeff Wheeler's sister."

Jeff Wheeler sounds familiar, but I still can't place it.

Then she adds, "He was adopting Rufus."

Ah, now it clicks in. Rufus was an adorable golden retriever puppy. Dogs I remember; people not so much. Jeff Wheeler adopted him from the Tara Foundation, a rescue organization that my friend Willie Miller and I run, which is named after my wonderful golden retriever. The events leading up to the adoption were unusual, to say the least.

"Is there something wrong with Rufus?"

"No, he's fine. I just picked him up. It's Jeff; oh, Mr. Carpenter, I . . . Jeff . . . needs your help."

"What's wrong?"

"He's been arrested for murder. He didn't do it; there's no way."

"Who is the victim?"

"Stanley Franklin."

Jeff Wheeler performed a heroic act a year ago.

If you're keeping score at home, that puts him one heroic act ahead of me, and I'm not likely to even things up anytime soon. That is, unless pissing off presiding judges in court qualifies.

Jeff was going to pick up his girlfriend . . . if I remember correctly her name was Lisa . . . who was working late at a building in Paramus. I think she was an accountant. He was approaching the building when an explosion took place; it was later determined to be caused by a gas leak.

He ran into the building, only to find the lobby engulfed in flames and the stairs completely impassable. The smoke inside the building was thick and choking. There was a dog, a golden retriever puppy, in a cage on the stairs and Jeff heard it barking. He grabbed it and ran out. There was nothing else he could do; no one else he could help.

Because the incident happened after eight o'clock in the evening, only seven people were inside, and all of them perished. Had it happened during business hours, the death toll would have been far worse, but this was bad enough. The victims included Jeff's girlfriend, and it was later revealed that he was going to propose to her during an upcoming vacation.

The dog, named Rufus, belonged to a colleague of Lisa's who also died in the incident. She had no family that wanted Rufus, so the county took charge of him.

But he was just a puppy and had not even had all his shots. There was a small parvo outbreak at the shelter at the time, and it was deemed too risky to bring him there, so he came to us at the Tara Foundation.

The media justifiably called Jeff a hero and Rufus got his fifteen minutes of fame as well. Rufus's survival was hailed as a miracle, and some over-the-top writers and commentators mentioned divine intervention. I'm not sure how the families of the seven deceased felt about that, since their relatives were apparently not worthy of that same heavenly help.

Willie Miller, his wife, Sondra, and I decided not to place Rufus right away; we would take a few weeks to make sure he was healthy and to give him time to receive his final shots. He had also inhaled a lot of smoke in the fire and needed some special treatment for his lungs.

After about a week, Jeff showed up. He could not get Rufus out of his mind and just felt that he had to have him. I guess that on some level Rufus represented a connection to Lisa, or maybe Jeff just loves dogs.

Willie spoke to him and ascertained how good a dog home Jeff's would be, and Willie signed off on it. He is strict when it comes to where our dogs wind up; if he thinks a home is a good one, I have no doubt it is.

But in our view Rufus needed a couple more weeks for

health reasons, so he stayed with us in our home. Jeff frequently came to visit and literally spent hours with Rufus, treating him to nonstop petting.

Once Rufus was ready, Jeff took him home, and that was the last I heard from him, except for occasional email updates telling us how well Rufus was doing.

So the news that Jeff has been accused of murdering Stanley Franklin is jarring and comes out of left field.

I don't know much about Stanley Franklin, only that he was one of the wealthier men in this area. I know he was heavily involved in real estate, and I believe he controlled a business that was the parent company of a number of smaller enterprises.

I think he was also in the news a few weeks ago for something to do with finding missing famous works of art, but I wasn't interested in that. I don't own any famous works of art, missing or otherwise. And my favorite Art is Garfunkel.

I saw on the news yesterday that Franklin was murdered, but I didn't pay much attention to that either. It had nothing to do with me and it didn't involve the NFL or the college football playoffs, so I switched channels.

I ask Carol a few more questions and say I will call her back. I need time to think about this; I am mostly retired and my goal for quite a while has been to remove the *mostly* from that description. For a variety of reasons, that has proven difficult to accomplish.

When I get off the phone to think it through, I soon discover I'm not the only one doing the thinking.

"You need to get involved, Andy."

Laurie is standing in the doorway, apparently having heard the conversation from my end, which was enough for her to understand what was going on.

"Why is that, exactly?"

"Because we both like Jeff, and Ricky liked him, and Willie liked him."

I nod. "Hmm. Let me try out that defense. 'Ladies and gentlemen of the jury, it doesn't matter what evidence you have heard throughout this trial because Jeff Wheeler is innocent. And how do I know that? Because not only do I like him, and not only does Laurie Collins like him, but Ricky Carpenter and Willie Miller like him!'"

Laurie frowns her annoyance with me. "I didn't say he was innocent, Andy. I didn't even say you should represent him. I said you should get involved."

"And that means . . . ?"

"You should talk to him. You should find out the facts of the case from both sides, and then you can decide. And if you don't want to take the case, you can help him find a good lawyer." She smiles. "Though not as good as you."

There are basically two possible ways for me to be "involved" in a murder case, at least at this stage.

One way is to read up on everything I can about the crime and then talk to contacts that Laurie and I have in law enforcement. Laurie, as an ex-cop in the Paterson PD, has more ability than me to accomplish this. Almost everyone in the police department that I know hates me, even more than they hate most defense attorneys.

Laurie, on the other hand, has not burned any bridges; she was well-liked back in the day and that has not changed at all. I'm sure her former colleagues cannot understand how she could possibly be married to me. Or live with me. Or tolerate me. Or not shoot me.

The other possibility is that I just go down to the jail and talk to Jeff. It would not be a fun hour or so, but I'd find out what I need to know, I could tell Laurie I had become involved, and that would be that.

So I have a choice between doing a lot of research, which falls under the category of work, or just talking to Jeff. Since I have become work averse, it's an easy call for me.

People have a reverence for work that I don't understand. Calling a person a hard worker is considered to be paying them a compliment. Yet work is not part of the natural order of things. We are born, we lie in a crib for a year or so, and the next thing you know we are supposed to be laying concrete and digging ditches.

Not working should be the goal, like it is for every other species in the animal kingdom, with the possible exception of beavers. So in my view there are three rungs on the ladder, starting at the bottom with *hard worker*, then *worker*, and then *nonworker*. I have spent my entire adult life trying to get to the top of that ladder.

I'll admit my views on this subject are not completely thought out, but I'm sticking to them.

Of course, I have a third choice about the prospect of getting involved in this case. I could just refuse and tell Laurie that it is my decision and my life and I will do or not do whatever the hell I want, and she should butt out.

There is more of a chance that I will buy a shovel and get to work on those ditches.

But the truth is that I did like Jeff when he was adopting Rufus; he struck me as an intelligent, fairly gentle person. Of course, at the time he was grieving the loss of his girlfriend, so that could certainly have had an effect on his personality and demeanor.

But my feelings about Jeff, plus my fear of Laurie, are the reasons I am here at the Bergen County Jail, in Hackensack, waiting to be brought in to meet with him. I had told Carol I would come down here, and she contacted him and found out that he would very much like that.

I told the people at the desk that I was his lawyer, which in no way commits me to anything, but ensures that I will be allowed to see him. It never happens quickly; defense lawyers are not exactly catered to here. But within twenty minutes I'm brought back to a meeting room, which is a relatively short time to be kept waiting.

I've been in this room many times, and as much as I hope to never be here again, I always seem to find my way back. It is barren . . . just a metal table and two metal chairs, with two more identical chairs back against the wall. There is not the slightest hint of warmth to it; I often leave here more depressed than enlightened.

Jeff is brought in by two guards. His hands are cuffed in front of him, but no shackles are on his legs. The guards bring him to the chair opposite me and he sits down, then one of the guards says to me, "We'll be right outside."

"I'm just glad we could share this time," I say, which draws sneers from both of them as they leave.

Once they leave, Jeff says, "Mr. Carpenter, thank you so much for coming. When I asked Carol to call you, I thought it was a long shot."

"She was very persuasive. But I don't want you to think this means I'm taking your case. Right now I'm just here as a friend."

He nods. "I understand. I'll respect whatever you decide."

"Do you have a lawyer right now?"

Another nod. "A public defender. When I heard how much a defense with a private attorney would cost . . . I do okay, but I don't have anywhere near that kind of money."

"Who is the lawyer they assigned to you?"

"I haven't met him yet, but Roger something . . . maybe Dandridge. I wasn't thinking very clearly when they told me. I'm supposed to meet him tomorrow, before the arraignment."

"How much do you know about why you were arrested?"

"They said it was for the murder of Stanley Franklin. That's really it. I don't know how he was killed or why. And I certainly don't know who did it. I had nothing to do with it; I swear."

"And you don't know why they arrested you?"

Jeff is quiet for a few moments and looks uncomfortable, as if he doesn't want to say what he has to say. "Maybe because I threatened him."

"Why did you do that?"

"Because I believe he killed Lisa and those other people in that building."

"Wasn't it a gas leak?"

He nods. "Yes, apparently, but I don't believe it was accidental."

"You think he arranged to blow up his own building?"

"I do."

"Why would he do that?"

"I don't know for sure. I've spent a year trying to figure it out."

I don't like where this is going. If Jeff had a grudge against Franklin to the point that he had threatened him, at the very least he would need a rational reason to hold that grudge. I haven't heard one yet.

"Jeff, you think he set off the explosion, which means you think he is a mass murderer. You need to tell me why you hold that view," I say in as challenging a way as I can. If he dodges the question again, I'm out of here.

"Lisa worked for Marstan, Franklin's company; she was a director in finance. In the days before she died, she told me that she and some of her colleagues were worried about something that involved him. She wouldn't tell me what it was; they agreed they wouldn't say anything to anyone before he had a chance to respond. But it was definitely something serious."

He's sitting up a little straighter as he talks and seems more intense. This is something he feels strongly about.

"It sounded like it might be criminal. She said a couple of them, including her, thought they should just call the police. But they were going to confront him with it that night and give him a chance to explain."

"Where was the confrontation going to be?"

"At the office where they all died. Franklin's office was there as well; it was the company headquarters."

"He was supposed to be there that night?"

"That's what she said. I told it to the police afterwards and they came back and said he denied it to them. Why would he lie about that?"

"I don't know. But it would be important to find that out."

"Will you help me?"

"I believe I will," I say, proving once again that my mouth has a mouth of its own. It did not consult with my brain before saying it, which is a major breach of the decision-making chain of command.

"Thank you. You have no idea how relieved I am. What about the public defender? How do I let him know?"

"I'll deal with that. I'll see you tomorrow at the arraignment."

"Do I have to do anything to prepare?"

"No. You'll be asked to enter a plea. I assume you want to plead not guilty?"

"Absolutely. I am not guilty, Mr. Carpenter."

"Andy."

He smiles. "Andy."

"But I want you to understand something. I will make an application for bail, but it will be denied. You're being charged with first-degree murder, and the fact that the victim is a wealthy, prominent citizen doesn't help."

"That matters?"

"It does, because it makes it a case the media is interested in. The public will be informed every step of the way, and it wouldn't look good if the man the prosecution thinks is the killer is released. They'll say you're a danger to the community and a flight risk."

He nods, obviously not pleased. "Okay, but you'll try?"

"I'll try."

"My sister has Rufus; I miss him already."

"She can take care of him?"

"Yes, I think so. If it becomes too much, I'll tell her to call you. She has two children and is a single mother, so her plate is full. But she loves Rufus."

"She has my number."

"Andy, what will I do if we lose? I can't live in here."

I don't bother telling him that the county jail, which is where we are, is like a Four Seasons compared to where he will go if convicted.

I nod. "So we need to win."

"You took his case? Already?" Laurie asks.

"I did."

"Are you a pod? What did you do with the real Andy Carpenter?"

We're sitting in the den with Ricky, our sixteen-year-old son, so we try to limit our work talk. I always envision him talking to some psychiatrist in the future about how he learned the intricacies of mass murder at home from his parents.

"I even surprised myself. But afterwards, when I thought about it, I realized something terrible."

"What?" she asks.

"I don't think I can verbalize it. It's too upsetting."

"Andy . . ."

"Okay, you're my family and you deserve to hear this. You ready? I'm a lawyer; that's what I do. Okay? I said it."

"You just figured out that you're a lawyer?" Ricky asks. "Haven't you always been one?"

"It's not an easy thing to come to terms with, son. I don't expect you to understand."

"So retirement is not for you?" Laurie asks.

"At the very least it seems to be a moving target."

"Okay then, you're a lawyer and it's time to start lawyering. What's our first step? The team?"

I nod. "Let's get them in for a meeting."

Just then the phone rings, and I see by the caller ID that it's Billy "Bulldog" Cameron, returning my call. Billy is the head of the public defender's office and has been for as long as I can remember. He earned the nickname Bulldog by starring as a wide receiver for Georgia.

"Please tell me you're taking the case," Billy says as soon as I answer.

"What case?"

"Doesn't matter. Any case. Whichever one it is, you'd be perfect for it. I was just saying to my staff that every case we have is ideal for Andy Carpenter. And they said, 'Yes, Bulldog, Andy Carpenter is a wonderful attorney.' Your ears must have been burning."

I have taken some cases off Billy's hands in the past, and he's always thrilled when I do. His office is understaffed and underfunded, so anytime he can get a case off his plate it's a win for him. But he's pouring it on this time even more than usual.

"Bullshit," I say.

"Yes, there's some of that. Which case?"

"Jeff Wheeler . . . the Franklin murder."

"There is a God."

"So you weren't eager to handle it?"

"What gave me away?"

"Can you get me the discovery right away? I want to read it before the arraignment tomorrow."

"Are you kidding? I would transcribe it onto parchment myself if that's what it takes."

"The worst part of this is how happy you are."

"Only because now Mr. Wheeler will get the outstanding defense that he deserves."

"More bullshit. Just send the discovery to my house, not the office."

"It's on the way."

With nothing to do but wait for it to arrive, I have time to do one of my favorite things . . . take the dogs for a walk through Eastside Park.

Tara, the golden retriever who stands head and paws above all other living creatures, past and present, and Hunter, a pug who worships the ground Tara walks on, both love to go on these walks as much as I do.

Sebastian, our basset hound, considers it to be exercise if he lifts his head to receive a biscuit. If he had an independent source of income, he would hire someone to chew the biscuits for him. But he has made clear that he thinks walks are for suckers. So he ambles into the backyard to do his "business."

I do my best thinking when I'm on these walks; somehow I'm more clearheaded and able to focus. Maybe I should have done this before meeting with Jeff Wheeler.

I often talk to the dogs while we walk. In the past people would think I was crazy, but now I'm sure they think I'm talking into a hidden microphone while wearing a hidden earpiece.

"Tara, I stepped in it again."

Tara is smart enough to understand that I'm not talking

about the stuff that she and Hunter leave on the ground and goes in the plastic bag I'm carrying. But she doesn't comment on it because she's a dog who barks and doesn't speak.

"I'm not sure I've ever taken a case while basically knowing nothing about it. But maybe I'll get off the hook and they'll find evidence that Jeff didn't do it and drop the charges."

Tara literally squats and metaphorically pisses on my optimistic take on the situation.

"Yeah, I know. I don't have that kind of luck."

I swear it looks like Tara nods at that. She knows the truth when she hears it.

Stanley Franklin was shot in the doorway of his home in Alpine, a wealthy community off the Palisades Interstate Parkway.

It is on the New Jersey side of the Hudson River, yet if you go a relatively short distance along that highway, you enter New York state without ever crossing the river. I am full of geographic insights like that.

According to the discovery, the murder happened one day after Jeff Wheeler confronted and threatened Franklin publicly in a Fort Lee restaurant.

Franklin's wife, Margaret, who was home at the time of the murder, said she heard her husband yell something like "What the hell are you doing here?," though she admits she could not be sure of the exact words. She did not hear any gunshots, but minutes later found his body.

A gun with a silencer, which was quickly determined to be the murder weapon, was found in a plastic bag placed in a dumpster less than two blocks from Jeff's home in Teaneck. More significant, there were other items in the bag that clearly had an attachment to Jeff, plus his DNA was all over it.

There no doubt was enough evidence to have warranted

Jeff's arrest; I'm surprised they haven't reinstated the death penalty and executed him already. There was also enough evidence, and it was found so easily, that it makes me suspicious as to how it got there.

I am not familiar with the players in the Bergen County justice system; my misery is usually confined to Passaic County. The judge is Danielle Eddings, and I know nothing about her. Certainly I will try to learn all I can, but there's one thing I can be sure of: she will not like me.

The prosecutor is Joel Dietz, and I'm not familiar with him either. But I have no doubt that for the high-profile murder of a prominent citizen, they would not assign an intern to handle the trial. Dietz's bosses must think he's good, so he probably is.

When I arrive in the courtroom, Jeff is already waiting at the defense table. He is in handcuffs, but he won't be when and if a trial is held. It would be prejudicial for the jury, but since there is no jury yet, that's not an issue.

I would argue that the cuffs should be removed because of the presence of the media, but I would have to do so in front of the media, which would call more attention to it.

I pat him on the shoulder and tell him to just look impassive the entire time and avoid reacting to anything. "When they ask you to stand and enter a plea, just say, 'Not guilty, Your Honor,' in a calm, straightforward way. Nothing dramatic."

He nods. "I understand."

Over at the prosecution table there are four people, all of whom I assume are lawyers. Two white guys, plus an African American man and a woman who might be Hispanic. They are covering all their diversity bases for the jury; when the trial starts, they'll probably also have an Eskimo standing by.

One of the men breaks loose from the group and comes over to me, holding out his hand. "You must be Andy Carpenter."

"I must."

"I'm Joel Dietz; I just heard you were taking over the case last night."

"Were you able to sleep?"

He smiles. "Like a baby." Then, "We should talk."

I return the smile. "Have your people call my people."

"I'll do that."

Actually, I do have people, or at least a person. His name is Eddie Dowd, a former New York Giants football player turned lawyer who works with me when we have a case. I didn't bother asking him to come here today because arraignments don't exactly require brilliant lawyering.

Judge Eddings comes in. She is younger than I expected, but attempts to make up for it with a stern, no-nonsense expression. Color me intimidated.

She welcomes all the lawyers, announces the case, and then Dietz summarizes the charges. Then she asks if there are any motions to be filed. I tell her that I only have one at the moment, but that is subject to change since I just took on the case.

Of course since the murder was committed only three days ago, there was no case to take on before that, but no one points out that obvious fact. I make a motion for bail to be granted and offer a house arrest and electronic monitoring.

"The community would be safe with that confinement, Your Honor. Mr. Wheeler has never before been charged with a crime, and to keep him incarcerated while awaiting trial is a punishment that denies him his presumption of innocence."

Dietz objects, terming Jeff a danger to the community and a flight risk, standard stuff, and the judge denies my motion. I can sense Jeff reacting next to me, even though I had warned him this was coming.

She asks Jeff to stand and enter a plea, and I stand with him. Jeff says, "Not guilty, Your Honor," and we sit back down. She sets a trial date that is sooner than I'd like, but further down the road than Jeff would like it to be.

Judge Eddings adjourns the session, and we're on our way.

Looking back, I haven't been on a lot of teams in my life.

I played on the baseball team for Eastside High School, but I was the weak link on a pretty terrible squad. I played shortstop, and though I was a barely adequate fielder, I had some hitting issues. I couldn't hit the curveball, or the fastball, or the slider, or the changeup. I don't think I could have hit .250 in T-ball.

The team I'm on now, our legal team, is damn good, if a bit unconventional. Though there is not a single person in the group that I would want to be in a foxhole with, that's only because foxholes are not my thing. I prefer places with room service and hopefully a casino.

When it comes to legal battles, I'll take these people anytime, which is what I'm thinking as I look around the room. We're in my office on Van Houten Street in Paterson, on the second floor above a fruit stand. Since I'm a summer-fruit guy, having the stand below the office is not that big a perk for me this time of year. Apples are not my thing.

The conference room is not big enough for a group this size, but it's bigger than my office. There are airport bathroom stalls bigger than my office.

Laurie is here, of course, as she is my lead investigator. Next to her is Eddie Dowd, one of two lawyers on the team, and the only one who actually wants to be a lawyer. As a tight end for the Giants who specialized in blocking, not pass-catching, he was extremely competent and not at all flashy, which describes his legal style as well.

Next to Eddie is Corey Douglas, like Laurie a Paterson PD ex-cop. Corey was a canine cop and retired with his partner and friend, a German shepherd named Simon Garfunkel. At the moment Simon is under the table at Corey's feet, munching on a chewie. Simon is not much for meetings; he prefers action.

To Corey's right is Sam Willis. Sam is an accountant, and his office is actually down the hall from mine. Sam is also a computer genius and master hacker, though he considers that term to be a bit crude. But Sam can hack into anything, and thus he is an invaluable investigator for us.

Next to Sam is Marcus Clark. I often describe Marcus as the scariest guy on the planet, but that seems limiting. I would also take him over anyone on any other planet in a steel-cage death match. Marcus is part of the investigative team with Laurie and Corey. When things get scary, and they sometimes do because when you take on murder cases there are murderers involved, Marcus is Vice President in Charge of Keeping Me Alive.

Next, between Marcus and me, is Edna. I'm not sure how to describe her position here. She considers herself the office manager; I used to think of her as my assistant, until I realized she doesn't actually assist me. Edna makes me look like a hard worker, but I put up with it because I like her, and because she's not that competent anyway.

Eddie basically deals with Edna on typing motions and stuff for court. Her all-time favorite invention is spell-check because it gives her a foil to blame typos on.

Not here is Willie Miller, my partner in the Tara Foundation, which is okay because he's not officially a part of this team. Willie sometimes pitches in when things get scary and violent; he's no Marcus, but he's tough and fearless.

"Our client is Jeff Wheeler," I say, as a way of calling the meeting to order. "He has been wrongly accused of killing Stanley Franklin." I can see Corey in a cross between a smile and a frown; as an ex-cop, Corey's default position is that the accused are usually guilty.

"Some of you may have heard of Franklin; he was a very wealthy businessman who owned about half of New Jersey. He also had a bunch of other businesses, which we need to learn as much as we can about. And I know he is a collector of expensive pieces of art. There was a big announcement about it a few weeks ago. Sam, can you get on that? Do a deep dive on him."

"Will do."

"I have some of the discovery; I'm sure there will be a lot more. You are all welcome and encouraged to read it." Edna winces at the thought; she'll probably try to find a CliffsNotes version.

"Franklin was shot in his home three nights ago. You'll see in the discovery why they arrested our client, and we will need to refute all of it.

"You may recall that Jeff Wheeler was near the scene when that building exploded in Paramus last year, killing seven people, including his girlfriend. He ran in and was able to save a golden retriever puppy, who he wound up adopting from us.

"Franklin owned that building, and Jeff believes that he intentionally destroyed it, making him a mass murderer. He has been outspoken about it and threatened Franklin the night before he died. It proved to be an ill-timed threat, in that it immediately made him a person of interest when Franklin got killed.

"But the reason that Jeff was a suspect is the same reason that he was a likely person to pin the blame on. The real killer knew that and engineered it all.

"I have no idea if Franklin had anything to do with the building explosion, and even if he did, it may well have nothing to do with our case. But we should look into it carefully anyway.

"Our firmly held position is that our client is innocent. But one thing we know with absolute certainty is that someone killed Stanley Franklin. We need to find out why, and we need to find out who.

"That's the only way we are going to win this thing."

I'm going to be looking for a reaction from Jeff, but what I'm worried about is my reaction to his reaction.

I'm back at the jail, about to confront him with the evidence that got the cops to charge him; it has not been shared with him yet. I'm interested to see what he says and how he acts when he hears it.

What I dread is my coming away from this with a feeling that he might in fact be guilty. I took the case based on a gut feeling; from the same gut that every spring makes me think the Giants are going to win the Super Bowl . . . the same gut that persuaded me to go to law school.

My gut has issues.

But what I don't want is to go through trial preparation and a trial in defense of a person who I think is a murderer. That is a horrible prospect and might in fact cause me to insist that Jeff find new counsel.

But I'm getting ahead of myself, particularly since my gut is also notoriously weak at determining when someone is lying or being insincere. I could completely misread Jeff's reaction, whatever it is.

Once Jeff is brought into the meeting room, I get right to it. I show him a photo of the plastic bag that was found in the garbage near his house. The photo was included with many others in the discovery material.

"Do you know what this is?" I ask, not really the best way to ask the question.

"A plastic bag."

"Do you recognize it?"

He looks puzzled, and I can't say I blame him. But he's not looking worried or guilty or scared; at least I don't think so.

"Do I recognize the plastic bag?"

"This was found in a garbage can about a block from your house."

"So?"

"So in it were a number of items. Do you recognize these?"

I show him another photograph from the discovery with the items in the bag spread out. I have cropped the photo on the left side, so it does not include the gun. In the photo are a few innocuous things like a scribbled grocery list, an empty M&M's wrapper, an advertisement for a Chinese restaurant, and an empty Starbucks coffee cup.

"Andy, I don't know why you're showing me this stuff. That's my garbage . . . the grocery list was mine. Where did you get it? And why is it important?"

I don't answer his question but add one of my own. "Do you recognize this?" I show him another copy of the same photo, but not cropped to exclude the gun.

"What the hell . . . Where did that gun come from?"

"The same plastic bag."

"Come on, what are you saying? That this is my gun?"

"Here's what I'm saying. The police found this plastic bag in a dumpster a block from your house. In it were all these items, including the gun and your DNA. And the gun is the one that was used to kill Stanley Franklin."

"That is not my gun. I don't own a gun and never have. What the hell is going on here?" Then, "Wait a minute . . . that must be the bag that was in my car. I keep a plastic bag on the passenger side of the car for me to throw papers and stuff in; otherwise my car is always a mess. Lisa taught me to do it. That could be the bag from the car. It must be, because after I do grocery shopping, I usually throw the list in that bag."

"And the gun?"

"There was no gun. I'm telling you there was no gun. Please believe that."

I almost want Jeff to excuse me for a moment so my gut and I can have a one-on-one conversation about how this is going. I know what my gut will say. He'll tell me that Jeff is coming off as completely believable, and that I should always trust my gut.

My defense attorney gut also tells me that the murder weapon being found near Jeff's house seems way too convenient; that he would have to be a moron to have set himself up that way.

So I'll tell my gut about all the times he's been wrong, and he'll tell me it's ultimately my call and responsibility. We've had this conversation a lot, and that's how it always ends.

My gut will never actually make a crucial decision because he's gutless.

Jeff is waiting for me to say something; he has no idea what is going through my warped mind. "Andy?"

"Okay, I believe you. But it's a fact that all of this was found near your house, and DNA has matched it to you, so we can't deny it."

"But I didn't put it there."

I nod. "Understood, but that means someone did. Someone who actually killed Franklin . . . someone who wants you to take the fall for it and made a plan to frame you."

"I don't know who that could be."

"Well, you'd better think about who it could be. Think hard; it may well be someone you know."

"Okay, I will."

"Since the explosion, on your crusade to pin the blame on Franklin, has anybody else been on your side, supporting your position?"

"Yes, a few family members of the other victims. But they may have been more interested in the money. The insurance company didn't pay nearly what they all thought they should, and if Franklin could have been shown to be negligent, or to have deliberately set off the blast, they could have all taken him for a fortune."

"Okay, make up a list of the people on that committee for me, with contact information if you have it."

"Will do."

"Have you talked to your sister? How's Rufus?"

"She says he seems lethargic. He's home alone a lot; I used to take him everywhere."

"He can stay at our house if she wants."

"Thanks, Andy . . . I'll tell her that."

Alpine is a wealthy town, with a per capita income of over $200,000.

Looking at Stanley Franklin's house from the street, I guess that $200,000 might have paid for the landscaping. Stanley Franklin and his wife lived very comfortably.

Laurie and I are here because one of the first things we always do is check out the scene of the crime. In this case we can't actually enter the scene; Franklin's wife, Margaret, refused the request we made through the prosecutor's office.

We could have insisted and the court would have backed us up, but there was no need to do so, at least not at this point. The shooting happened at the front door, and we can see that door quite well from this vantage point.

There is a healthy distance between the houses in this neighborhood, making it less likely that a neighbor would have seen anything, and there is a long path up to the front door. For the killer to have just walked up, rung the bell, and fired the shot took a lot of confidence and a cold-blooded nature that feels a bit chilling.

"No streetlights," Laurie says, looking up.

"That's fairly common in high-class neighborhoods," I

say. "The residents think that being able to see ruins the ambience."

"Made it easier for the killer to have gotten away unseen."

"The cops canvassed the neighborhood and came up blank."

"Do we think he just pulled up in his car, got out, walked to the front door, and killed Franklin?" Laurie asks.

"His wife did not report seeing a car. She also didn't know where the killer went when he left the house."

"I'm sure she was focused on her dying husband."

"He was shot in the back. The police theory is that he answered the door, saw who the visitor was and that he was holding a gun, then turned and tried to get away. He was shot twice about eight feet from the door."

"If it was me, I wouldn't have parked right here," Laurie says. "I'd have parked at least a block away. There was always a chance that Franklin's wife would have seen the car and maybe even the license plate."

Laurie points. "That sign says permit parking only after six P.M. We should check and see if any cars were ticketed that night within a five-block radius of here."

"We should be so lucky."

She nods. "A definite long shot. But maybe one of these rich people didn't like a car parked in front of their house, maybe they saw that as another ambience killer. They could have called the cops."

"We should ask Corey to ask neighbors within that radius to see if they saw anything."

"Good idea, but we can narrow it down some."

"How?" I ask.

"He can focus on the streets west of here, towards the highway. The killer would want to get out of the area as fast as possible. Once he reached the highway, he was home free. If he was even slightly smart, he would reduce the driving necessary to get there."

"Good point. Plus the hospital is in the other direction. By parking towards the highway, he'd be sure not to run into the first responders."

"So according to the discovery, Franklin's wife heard him talk to the killer?" Laurie asks.

"Yes."

"So she must have been close by and could conceivably have seen him. The killer could have easily shot her as well, to remove the possibility of her identifying him. But he didn't."

"You think she could have been involved?" I ask.

"I would never say that, not without evidence. There are too many other possibilities. The shooter might not have seen her, since she couldn't see him. She said she was in the bedroom. Or maybe he was wearing a mask and therefore wasn't worried about being identified. There are a hundred other scenarios in which he wouldn't shoot her."

"I feel like Franklin knew the killer," I say.

"Why?"

"For one thing, his wife said he asked the killer, 'What are you doing here?' That's not the way you would speak to a stranger, or intruder. That's what you say to someone you know but are surprised to see.

"For another, there might be a peephole in that door, or he could have looked out those little windows on the side. Either way you don't just open the door at night, in this neighborhood, unless you know who is on the other side."

"He knew Jeff," Laurie points out.

"But Jeff threatened him and had been accusing him of mass murder for a year. I'm not sure Franklin opens the door when he sees him."

"Hopefully you're right."

"Hopefully the jury will think I'm right."

"There are two main possibilities, as I see it."

I've called Laurie, Corey, Eddie Dowd, and Sam in to have what might generously be called a brainstorming session; with the little knowledge we have at this point, it's not going to be much of a storm.

"The first is that Stanley Franklin was the target and Jeff is the patsy. He was a known enemy of Franklin, and when he threatened him, he became a perfect setup target.

"The second is that it all somehow relates to the building explosion. Maybe Jeff was right and Franklin did it himself, with accomplices. Those accomplices saw Jeff causing trouble and maybe leading to a reexamination of what happened. To protect themselves, they killed Franklin and got Jeff out of the way at the same time."

"Why would they kill Franklin if he was their partner?"

I shrug. "File that under 'I have no idea.' Maybe Franklin wasn't a full partner, maybe he was taking orders and was no longer considered reliable. Or it could have been a bunch of other reasons still to be uncovered."

"The first option is far more likely," Laurie says, and I agree with that. "Jeff threatening Franklin put a neon light over his head that said, 'You can blame me.'"

"There is a third possibility," Corey says. "It's just possible that our client is guilty."

"It doesn't help us to think that way," I say. "He says he's innocent, he's pleading not guilty, so that's our position. The entire state of New Jersey is taking the other side."

Corey nods. He understands the role that the defense plays, though his cop mind still clearly views Jeff's guilt as the most likely possibility. The good news is that it won't affect his work; he's demonstrated that many times.

"Sam, I need you to find out whatever you can about the explosion," I say. "Every aspect, including the financial ramifications."

"Will do."

"And Eddie," I say, "there's nothing in the discovery about the explosion because it doesn't relate to the case in the prosecution's mind. I doubt it would even have been treated as a potential criminal matter, so no criminal case file would have been opened by the police or prosecutor's office. They operated from the beginning on the idea that the explosion was an accident, a gas leak.

"But there would have been a thorough investigation by the fire department, and there must be documents and information created in the process. We need to get the judge to authorize a subpoena for all relevant material."

"Should not be a problem," Eddie says. "If the prosecution is using it to demonstrate motive, then it's obviously relevant."

"Good. Of course, whether Jeff is right or wrong about Franklin's culpability will not carry the day in this case. The motive, in their view, is the fact that Jeff *believed*

Franklin to have been guilty, and to have killed his girlfriend and others by deliberately causing the blast.

"Their position is that it doesn't matter if he was right or wrong, though obviously they think he was wrong. They want Franklin to look as much like an innocent victim as possible. But either way, it's how he felt and what he believed. That belief is the motive."

"Understood," Eddie says.

Sam says, "So I've got some information on Franklin. Not a lot, just preliminary stuff, but . . ."

"Let's hear it, Sam."

"Okay, he had his hand in a lot of different things, all under the parent company, called Marstan Industries. It's obviously a combination of Margaret, his wife, and his own name, Stanley."

"Our company would be called And-ie Industries," I say.

Laurie does a double take. "Excuse me?"

"It would be the *And* in *Andy* and the *ie* in *Laurie*."

She shakes her head. "I'm thinking Laurand Industries."

"Come on, that has no ring to it, no cachet."

She smiles. "As the president of the company, I'll name it whatever I want."

Good point. "Yes, Madam President."

"Can we move on?" Corey asks.

"Sorry," I say. "Sam, what does Marstan do?"

"A better question would be what don't they do. They own a lot of real estate, but most of it is dedicated to their own businesses. They have a bunch of fast-food restaurant franchises, mostly Wendy's with a few Buffalo Wild

Wings thrown in, a chain of mall jewelry stores, and some of those mass-market dental offices, mostly on the West Coast.

"Then they have movie theaters in the Midwest, a chain of thirty-five low-cost hair salons, and even some hotel franchises, all Hiltons, mostly near airports. Their other main business is importing, both for their own businesses and for others that contract them."

"All of these things make money?" Laurie asks.

"I'm not there yet. Franklin had a minority partner in all this, a guy named Wilson Paul."

"Not Paul Wilson?" Corey asks.

Sam smiles. "No, his first name is a last name and vice versa. Must have had obnoxious parents." Then, "Stanley Franklin was also an art collector; he was somewhat famous in that world and that seems to be his passion in life. He's done many interviews on the subject, mostly in art magazines but also a few mainstream.

"His own collection is worth a lot of money, but he also would find famous paintings all over the world and make sure that auction houses got them. Some of them he'd buy himself, but most would be purchased by others. A few weeks ago he announced with an auction house a new discovery of a bunch of paintings the Nazis hid. It's a big deal in that world."

"I saw that," Laurie says.

"Just curious . . . was any of his art destroyed in the explosion?" I ask.

Sam nods. "According to media reports, absolutely. I'll access the insurance settlement and find out the details."

Corey winces slightly. Sam's breaking into these records is clearly illegal, and it offends Corey's cop sensibility, though he's getting used to Sam's efforts like this. Laurie used to have the same ethical issue about it, but she's already come over to our side. She didn't get to be president of Laurand Industries without cutting corners.

Sam's work in this area is often helpful to us, particularly in saving time and for convenience. Any relevant information he gets we can always get a subpoena to collect, but this kind of searching in advance tells us what to ask for with precision and, most important, gets that information to us faster.

"Okay, whatever you can find out. I doubt there are too many mass murders in the fine-art world; if someone wants revenge against someone, I suspect they just outbid them. But we need to cover all our bases."

Sam nods. "Got it."

I turn to Laurie. "Have Marcus ask around with his contacts about the Franklin murder and the explosion. This doesn't sound like it's connected to the kind of people that Marcus generally deals with, but you never know."

"Okay."

"Is Marcus around? He's not invading North Korea or anything?"

"I'm sure he's around and waiting."

"Good. That's a wrap. Let's get some information to go on."

The Paramus Fire Department is an all-volunteer unit, which is amazing to me.

These are people who go through intense training to risk their lives, sometimes in severe heat and high humidity, sometimes in freezing temperatures, all to save the homes and possessions and lives of their neighbors.

They are selfless and dedicated to a life of public service. I am the same way, except for the selfless, dedicated, life-risking, public-service part.

Captain Lee Hornstein is the head of one of four teams of firefighters. Corey is a good friend of his going back to high school, so Corey set up this meeting for me with Captain Hornstein at the firehouse.

Hornstein is one of those people who seems immediately likable, and firefighters don't generally share with police the built-in hatred for defense attorneys. So he's smiling at me; the only cop to smile at me in the last five years was giving me a speeding ticket.

After our hellos, Hornstein asks me how Corey is doing. "I have to admit, I didn't see him moving into defense work. And I thought Simon Garfunkel would have bitten a defense attorney before working for one," he says, referring to Corey's dog.

"My dog Tara vouched for me with Simon, which went a long way."

He nods. "Makes sense. How can I help you?"

"You worked on the building explosion last year?" I don't have to further identify it; Paramus has remarkably few building explosions.

"I did. One of the more unpleasant episodes in my career. It was the fire and smoke that killed the people more than the blast. Some of those bodies . . ."

He doesn't finish the sentence, which is fine with me. "The cause was determined to be from a gas leak?" It's a statement asked as a question.

"Yes."

"Any chance that's wrong?"

"None."

"Gas is just gas."

Before I can go on, he interrupts and smiles. "Very true and very profound."

I laugh. "Thank you. But it doesn't explode on its own, right? Something has to happen to detonate it? A match, a spark?"

"Also true."

"So what set this one off?"

"Absolutely no way to know, and we tried to find out, believe me."

"Could it have been intentional?" I ask.

"No way to know that either. There was no evidence

that was the case, but an explosion of that intensity leaves few clues."

"But you ruled it accidental?"

"Not exactly; we ruled it of indeterminate origin. The fact that the gas leaked is beyond question. The specific causes of both the leak itself and the detonation were not addressed other than to say they were unknowable. Post-explosion analysis is not an exact science."

"Did the police get involved?"

He shrugs. "As I recall, they asked me for my conclusions, and I told them what I just told you. They most likely decided that there was therefore no reason to consider it a criminal event, which would have been the correct decision, based on the available information."

"And there was valuable artwork destroyed as well?"

He nods. "Yes, apparently. There was a studio on the top floor devoted to it. It did not fare well in the blast. The insurance company was all over it, but it didn't affect our work. We were concerned with why it happened, not what was damaged or destroyed."

"Could the artwork have been removed before the explosion? Was it definitely there?" I ask this because it's hard to make the case that Franklin, an avid art lover, would willingly blow up what must have been fine works of art.

Hornstein shrugs. "The insurance company must have been satisfied that it was there, or I would have heard about it."

"Were you aware that some people felt Stanley Franklin was himself responsible?"

"By some people you mean your client?" Hornstein asks.

"Yes."

"I think I heard that at some point, but that's not really an area I get into. I report the facts as I see them; I have no idea about the motivations of people that are involved. It doesn't affect the facts on the ground."

"So if I said that it was deliberately done . . ."

"I couldn't say you were wrong, or right. All I can do is look at the information I have on hand. The motivations and placing the blame on specific individuals . . . that's the job of the police . . . and apparently the attorneys."

"How many gas leak explosions have you seen in your time doing this?"

"In nineteen years, three."

"So if it was an accident, it was a rare one."

He smiles. "I feel like I'm testifying and you're trying to maneuver me."

I return the smile. "Guilty as charged."

"Let's put it this way, if it was deliberately done, after what I saw, I hope you find the son of a bitch and put him away for the rest of his life."

If their offices are any indication, Marstan Industries has recovered quite well from the explosion.

It is headquartered in a six-floor building that they rebuilt on the site where the incident took place, and it is sleek and modern. It's remarkable that it was built so fast; it must have cost Marstan big money to get it done.

There are two female receptionists who look exactly alike sitting in front of consoles that resemble the ones Captain Kirk used to peer at. And in keeping with the theme, the elevators that take me up to the sixth floor are so fast that they must have been designed by NASA.

When the elevator door opens, there is a woman who looks so much like the two receptionists downstairs that it's possible the company breeds them. Like the two downstairs, she is smiling and friendly. She asks me to follow her to Mr. Paul's office, which I am happy to do, since I'm here to see Mr. Paul.

I'm ushered into Wilson Paul's office, and he is the first unsmiling person I've run into. He is sitting behind his desk and doesn't bother getting up to shake my hand when I enter. I'm just not feeling the love.

The office is nothing short of spectacular, large and

elegantly furnished, with vases of fresh flowers on three different tables. The back wall is all glass, with as good a view as you can have, considering this is Paramus and not Paris.

The nonglass walls have six paintings on them. I'm not into fine art, but these look like they weren't bought at Walmart.

"Mr. Carpenter."

"Mr. Paul," I say, since we're apparently in the name announcing phase of the conversation. "Thanks for seeing me."

"We are not on the same side."

"Of the desk?"

"Of more than that. I only agreed to meet with you to find out how you intend to get that killer off."

"The facts will do the work. You are not a believer in the presumption of innocence?"

"I am not a believer in murderers getting off on technicalities. Your reputation precedes you."

I frown. "That always happens. I ask it not to; I explain that we should enter rooms at the same time, but reputations seem to have a mind of their own. At least that's their reputation."

He isn't amused. "Get to your questions and I'll decide if I'll answer them."

"I hope you will. Informal sessions like this are much preferable to a deposition." It's a subtle threat and a mostly empty one; it's unlikely the judge would let me depose him, at least at this stage. But most nonlawyers don't realize that.

"Let's move it along."

I nod. "Will do. You were Stanley Franklin's partner?"

"Minority partner. Stanley and his wife, Margaret, owned, and she still owns, ninety percent of the company. I own the other ten."

"But you ran it together?"

"Yes, in that regard we were full partners. Stanley had faith in me, and he had other interests outside of this business."

"His art collection?"

Paul nods. "He was an avid connoisseur and collector."

"But you're not?"

"How is that relevant?"

"To be honest, I'm not big on relevance at this stage of a case. I'm all about collecting information and figuring out later if it's useful."

"To be equally honest, I don't really care what you're big on." Then, "I appreciate fine art, but not at the level of expertise, or even interest, that Stanley had. Very few people are at that level."

"Some valuable paintings of his were destroyed in the explosion, as I understand it?"

"So I'm told; I was more concerned with our people."

"At the time the explosions happened, there were seven of your employees in the building. Is that an unusually large number for that time of night?"

He nods. "Unfortunately, yes. There was a late meeting called to deal with some supposed crisis."

"Do you know that that crisis was?"

"No, and it doesn't matter. Nothing mattered in light

of what happened. Events like that make one realize what is important; we lost some wonderful people. Business problems pale in comparison."

"I understand. But it was not a meeting that you or Stanley Franklin needed to attend?"

"I didn't even know it was happening; I doubt very much if Stanley did either."

"So he wasn't supposed to be there?" Franklin's expected attendance is something that Jeff claims Lisa told him.

"I just told you I doubt if he knew it was happening."

"The people that were working, and that died, were all in the accounting department?"

"Finance."

"Did you investigate how the explosion happened?"

"The authorities did . . . along with the insurance company. Our efforts were not needed nor solicited in that regard."

"Is Mrs. Franklin going to get involved in the activities of the company?" I like to jump around in my questioning.

"Hard to say; she's just lost her husband, so I would think the business is not top of mind right now. For the time being, she has asked to be kept informed of anything that requires her attention and has expressed her trust in me and my colleagues to run it as we did before."

"Business doing well?"

"Quite."

"I ate at a Taco Bell the other day . . . so I'm doing my part."

"Unless the one you ate at was in the Midwest, we didn't benefit from it."

"That seems far to go for a soggy chalupa."

"Are we done here?" he asks.

"For the time being."

Nick Edwards answered on the cell phone that never received calls from anyone other than this one person.

The caller ID always identified it as coming from various states, never the same one twice. Edwards did not believe the caller was actually in those states; based on his accent, he probably wasn't even in the country. But he clearly had a way to mask the origin of his calls.

The caller had made Edwards a fairly rich man these last couple of years, at least by his previous standards. Yet he had never actually told Edwards his name. He told Edwards to call him Sir, and Edwards had always complied. Sir was the kind of guy whose orders one obeyed.

Edwards was a scary, violent person, but he instinctively felt he was not in Sir's class in that area. Perhaps it was because the man was so soft-spoken and calm while directing violent actions. So Edwards did as he was told, made his money, and did not ask questions.

Sir never said hello or engaged in small talk of any kind; he always got right to the point. It was the only thing about him that Edward liked, besides the money.

"Carpenter met with Wilson Paul," Sir said.

"So? What's the problem?"

"Did I give you the impression that the purpose of this call was for us to engage in a strategic give-and-take?"

"No. Sorry."

"I want to know who else he meets with."

"Carpenter? Or Paul?"

"Carpenter."

"You want me to follow him?"

"Yes."

"Okay. I can do that."

"At eight P.M. each day, I will call you and you can tell me what you've learned."

"No problem. I'm doing this at the regular rate?"

"Yes."

"Sounds good to me," Edwards says, but he doubted that Sir heard him because the line was dead.

What Edwards didn't know was that Sir was troubled by where this was going. Sir had originally not wanted to involve Wheeler in this situation at all, but had allowed himself to become convinced.

Had they not implicated Wheeler, the investigation into Franklin's death would be growing cold by now, instead of being intensified by Carpenter and those working with him. It was far more dangerous now than it would have been.

But it would not be long before the whole thing would be behind him, and his goal, the one he had dreamed of since arriving in this country with nothing all those years ago, would be accomplished.

He would be the highest bidder for the artwork at Echelon, and then nothing would ever be the same.

I used to go to Charlie's Sports Bar and Restaurant almost every night.

Then and now there was always a game to watch on one of the dozens of TV screens in the place. There were only two exceptions to that: the nights before and after the Major League Baseball All-Star Game. Nothing is played on those nights; not baseball, football, basketball, or hockey. As far as I am concerned, those nights have no reason to exist.

These days I only come here to Charlie's maybe once or twice a week. Things changed when I married Laurie, and again when we adopted Ricky. I found I had more of a desire to be home, and since I cannot be in two places at once, Charlie's took a backseat.

The same thing is not true of the two friends with whom I have always shared our regular table here, Pete Stanton and Vince Sanders. Pete is captain in charge of the Homicide Division of the Paterson Police Department, and Vince is editor of the local newspaper.

Pete and Vince have things in common. They are both sports degenerates, as am I, and neither have paid for a meal or drink in Charlie's in years. That is because I, being wealthy and a sucker, get stuck with the tab, even when I am not present. I pay that tab monthly, and the way they eat and drink, I could be paying in gold bullion.

When I do show up, we don't miss a beat; we eat burgers, drink beer, watch sports, and insult each other during time-outs and halftimes. Sometimes I'll ask Pete questions seeking information regarding a case I'm working on, but there is little hope that I'll get anything positive tonight, since the Franklin murder did not take place in Paterson, and therefore Pete is not involved.

"Do you know a cop named Carl Richardson?" I ask. He's a homicide detective in Alpine who the discovery documents identified as the lead investigator on the Franklin case.

"Yeah, I know him," Pete says. "He's a good cop. Is he the lead on your case?"

"Yeah."

"He knows what he's doing, which means you don't have a prayer. Your boy is going down, which he should since he's guilty."

"You're familiar with the case?"

"No."

"Then once again you haven't the vaguest idea what you are talking about. My *client*, not my *boy*, is innocent. He is so innocent I'm surprised that you weren't the dope to make the arrest."

"Be careful or I'll have to arrest myself for strangling you," Pete says.

"Yeah? How'd you like to start paying for your own food? You and your cheap, slovenly friend here."

The cheap, slovenly friend, Vince, speaks up whenever the prospect of paying a check sends him into a panic. "Pete, apologize to our dear friend Andy."

"Never."

"Did either of you two losers know Stanley Franklin?" I ask.

"No," Pete says.

But Vince nods. "I talked to him on the phone once. We were running a piece on him last year and he called to warn me. Seemed like a pretentious asshole."

"Then you two must have had a lot in common," Pete says.

Vince and I both ignore that, and I ask, "Warn you about what?"

"He originally thought it was going to be a puff piece about him being a local, highly successful businessman and art collector. As I recall, our writer was asking the kind of questions that worried him and made him concerned about what would be in the story."

"What kind of things?"

Vince shrugs. "Beats me . . . I don't remember. I'm not sure I ever knew the details."

"So what did you tell him?"

"Same thing I tell everyone who tries to dictate to us: kiss my ass. We write what we want to write."

Pete frowns. "Yeah . . . drivel and horseshit."

Both Vince and I look at Pete and simultaneously decide to ignore him again. "Did the story run?" I ask.

"No. The reporter couldn't lock down the juicy stuff, so we didn't print it."

"Can I talk to your reporter?"

"I'm not sure; there might be ethical considerations."

"First of all, you wouldn't know an ethical consideration if you tripped and fell on one. Second of all"—I point to Pete—"is it ethical for you and J. Edgar Bozo over here to mooch off a local lawyer for years?"

"Now that I think of it, ethics are in the eye of the beholder," Vince says. "And my beholding eyes now tell me it's fine for you to meet with my writer."

A ringing doorbell is almost as bad as a ringing telephone; in some ways it is worse.

In a best-case scenario, it is someone who came to the wrong house; that way the interaction is brief and everyone goes on with their life.

Another decent outcome is that it is someone selling something, or trying to get me to vote for a candidate, or hoping to convert me to their religion. It's the in-person version of a telemarketer. This can be handled with a quick "Thank you, but I'm not interested," and again the intrusion is short-lived.

The worst is when someone I know shows up unannounced, just "popping in" to say hello. There is no defense to that. I have to invite them in and engage in the kind of small talk that I dread on the phone, times ten. Unlike the phone version, there is no way to use a conversational pause to end the interaction.

It is a social nightmare, with no way to avoid it. You can't screen an in-person visit the way you can screen a call; it's possible that the visitor has seen you through the window or heard the television or other signs of life. And the visitor won't be able to leave a message on a machine, so he or she would be more inclined to wait for the door to open.

In this case, everyone in the neighborhood has heard Laurie's insufferable Christmas music; it penetrates through walls and doors, so visitors know when we are home. It's yet another reason for me to hate Bing Crosby.

So this time I go to the door and answer it, cringing as I do. It's a woman who I do not recognize, holding a beautiful golden retriever on a leash. If I had to pick my absolute favorite living creature to be at the door when I open it, it would be a golden retriever.

"Hello," the woman says, and when I hesitate while trying to place her, she adds, "I'm Carol Hendrickson."

It clicks in and I say, "Carol . . . hello." Then, "Rufus, you have really grown up."

I invite her in and she enters just as Laurie comes in from the kitchen. "Andy, did you answer . . ." She stops when she sees our visitors, and I introduce them.

"So this is Rufus?" she asks. "What a handsome young man he's become."

We invite Carol into the den, but Rufus doesn't join us, since our dogs have discovered him and are sniffing away at one another.

"I'm sorry to barge in on you like this . . . I should have called."

"It's fine," Laurie says. "What can we do for you?"

Carol turns to me. "You said to tell you if Rufus became too much, and Jeff said the same. It's not Rufus; he's the absolute best. But with two small kids, and my working, he's just not getting the attention he deserves."

"We are delighted to have him," Laurie says, beating me to the punch.

One can never have too many golden retrievers. I'll speak to Tara, but I'm sure she'll be fine with it. Hunter will go along with whatever Tara wants, and Sebastian will be sound asleep most of the time so he won't even know Rufus is here.

As if on cue, Rufus, Tara, and Hunter come into the den. Tara looks at me quizzically as if to ask, "What's going on?"

"Tara, you remember Rufus? He's going to bunk here for a while," I say.

"I can't thank you enough," Carol says. "And Jeff will be very happy about this."

"It's our pleasure," Laurie says.

Carol stares at Rufus. "It's so horrible to picture him in that cage, smoke and flames everywhere. Jeff did such a wonderful thing to save him."

While I agree with that statement wholeheartedly, that's not what I'm thinking about at the moment, though I decide to wait until Carol leaves to verbalize it.

That takes about ten minutes. Carol declines Laurie's offer of coffee or something to eat, and after some small talk and my gentle refusal to give her a prediction about the outcome of Jeff's case, she leaves.

"You seem preoccupied," Laurie says. "I hesitate to ask, but what's going on in that lawyer's head of yours?"

"I'm wondering what Rufus was doing there that night."

"At the office when the explosion happened? His owner had brought him to work. Plenty of people do that."

"I know. That's not what I mean. Why was he in a cage in the lobby? Who brings their dog to their office and does that? Why leave him down there?"

"Maybe he was being disruptive. Or maybe the person's boss didn't want him there."

"If either of those were true, the person wouldn't have brought him in the first place."

"So what's your point?"

"Maybe whatever meeting they were having upstairs was unusual, or maybe someone was coming, someone who might not be pleased with the presence of a dog."

"You mean like the boss, Stanley Franklin?"

"Exactly. Jeff said that Lisa mentioned the meeting was important, and that Franklin was coming."

"And you think Rufus being in a cage in the lobby is evidence of that?"

I point to Rufus. "Would you put a dog like that in a cage? Remember what an adorable puppy he was?"

She smiles. "There is no chance I would put him in a cage, then or now."

"I rest my case."

Cynthia Wilmore was a colleague of Lisa Dozier's and one of the seven victims in the explosion.

She was also Rufus's original owner. He was just a puppy at the time, and she had brought him to work on that fateful day. Her family lived out West . . . I believe in California . . . and they had no interest in taking Rufus to live with them after Jeff rescued him. I would have no interest in being in a family like that.

After he was rescued, he came to our foundation, then Jeff adopted him, and the rest is history.

Laurie has located a woman named Jenna Landry, who was a neighbor and close friend of Wilmore's. They lived in the same apartment building in Fort Lee. It's an eleven-story building, so I'm not sure how Laurie found Landry, but maybe that's why she is an investigator and I'm not.

Laurie did not mention anything to her about Jeff or the Franklin murder; she simply said that I was investigating the explosion and that she might have some information that could be helpful. Landry was quite willing to talk to me, which is why her doorman has just sent me up to the sixth floor to her apartment.

"You're Andy Carpenter, the lawyer, right?" she asks after she lets me in.

"I'm afraid so." It should not have come as a surprise, since Laurie told her she'd be meeting with Andy Carpenter, a lawyer.

"I've heard of you; I even think I've seen you on television. You're a celebrity."

"It's not all it's cracked up to be."

We head to her kitchen for coffee and some kind of cake that she says is homemade. The coffee is weak and not hot enough, and the cake is considerably worse. It's the color of chocolate but without the taste.

But I put up with it; such is the price of fame.

After I tell her how delicious the cake is, she asks how she can help me. "I wanted to talk to you about Cynthia Wilmore."

She nods sadly. "She was wonderful; there isn't a day that goes by that I don't miss her."

"You were good friends?"

"Oh, yes. We worked together for three years, before Cynthia went over to Marstan. She's the reason I moved into this building; she was here before me and convinced me to come here."

I smile. "Did you ever meet Rufus?"

"Of course. He was the most adorable puppy. I always wondered what happened to him. Do you know if he got a good home?"

"I do. Mine."

"Wonderful. Is that why you're here? To talk about Rufus?"

"In a way, but the explosion is also peripherally related to another case I'm working on."

"What a horrible time that was."

"Did you know if Cynthia took Rufus to work frequently?"

"Oh, yes. Every day, except if she knew there was going to be a big meeting with outside people, or with her bosses. She loved that dog and wanted to take him everywhere."

"Did you ever visit her at work when Rufus was there?"

She nods. "Yes, a few times. He was the star of the office; everybody loved him and brought him treats."

"Did she keep him in a cage?"

"A cage?" she asks in obvious surprise. "No, of course not."

"He was rescued from a cage in the lobby when the explosion happened."

"I don't understand that. And why the lobby? He was always with her."

"Maybe someone was going to be there and she didn't want that person to see Rufus?"

"I guess that's possible. I think she once mentioned that one of the bosses made a comment about her bringing him to the office, so she was careful about it when he was going to be on her floor."

"Was the boss Stanley Franklin?"

"I don't know; I don't think she said."

"Did Cynthia like working at Marstan?"

"At first she did, but then . . . I don't know if I should say, she told me in confidence."

"I don't think that matters now," I say gently.

She nods. "I guess not, but she was a friend, and . . . she liked it there a lot, until near the end. She told me she was planning to leave."

"Did she say why?"

"No, she didn't want to talk about it. But something was bothering her; it was causing her a lot of stress."

"Something about the company?"

"I think so, yes."

"But you don't know what it was?" I find that sometimes if I ask the same question twice, I get an answer the second time.

This is not one of those times. "No. She wouldn't tell me, but it must have been important, because we told each other everything."

Gerald Shuler lost his wife, Cassie, in the blast at the Marstan building.

Jeff told me that Gerald was active in the effort to get as much money as possible as compensation for the loss. It was not something Jeff was particularly interested in, admittedly because as just a boyfriend he had no claim to anything.

So Jeff said that they clashed somewhat because of their different goals. Shuler, while legitimately grieving, was clearly out for the money. Jeff was more focused on showing that Franklin was criminally liable for what happened.

Shuler owns Pirelli's, an Italian restaurant in Teaneck. He's owned it for ten years, ever since purchasing it from the founder, who was named . . . wait for it . . . Pirelli.

He's agreed to meet with me at 4:00 P.M. at the restaurant, before the evening rush. I've never eaten here, but as soon as I walk in, I make a mental note to try it sooner rather than later. The smell of garlic is in the air, and if there is a better aroma than that, I don't know what it is.

One of the waiters is in the dining room when I arrive, and he heads to the kitchen to get Shuler for me. After a few minutes, Shuler comes out, wearing an apron and a chef's hat, the latter of which he takes off.

"You do the cooking?" I ask.

He smiles. "When the real chefs let me butt in. It's a love of mine."

"Is that garlic bread I smell?"

"No, we don't bake that until later. But believe me, it's worth waiting for."

We sit down and he says, "So you're representing Wheeler?"

He already knows the answer to that, since I told him so when I called him. "Yes."

"I guess he told you we disagreed a lot."

"No," I lie. "We didn't get into it much; I'm just covering all my bases."

He nods. "Well, we definitely disagreed on the approach. The families of the victims formed a pretty close group. To be totally honest, I didn't think Jeff even should have been a part of it."

"Why is that?"

"Well, he and Lisa weren't married; they weren't even engaged. So he wasn't technically a family member. And he therefore had no financial stake in the outcome. Legally, I mean."

I nod. "I understand."

"Look, I don't want you to think this was all about money. It wasn't. We were all in pain; we all lost someone we loved, senselessly. But money is the way you keep score in this country. What else did we have? Were we going to demand an apology from a leaking gas pipe?"

"So you don't think Franklin had any part in it?"

Shuler frowns. "You sound like your client. There was no evidence of it . . . none."

"Did your wife talk about any issues at work in the days or weeks before she died? Anything she might have been worried about?"

"No. I mean there were the usual stresses, but nothing unusual to speak of."

"Did she happen to mention whether Franklin was supposed to be there that night?"

"Not to me. But I was spending a lot of time getting the restaurant back on its feet; we had a rough time with COVID and all. So we didn't spend as much time together as I would have liked. I sure regret that now."

"Did you ultimately get the money you felt you were entitled to?"

"No, the insurance company lowballed us. And Franklin never stepped up. I don't like to speak ill of the dead, but he was a son of a bitch. I'm embarrassed to say I wasn't sorry to hear Jeff killed him."

"He didn't."

"Well, someone did."

I nod. "We can agree on that."

"Marstan has gone through some tough times," Sam says.

He continues his report on the research he's been doing. "COVID hit them really hard. People weren't going out to their restaurants, weren't going to the malls to buy jewelry, and weren't traveling and staying in their hotels. They laid off a bunch of people, but that was just a Band-Aid."

Sam has come over to give me his report on his deep dive into everything Stanley Franklin. Sam caught me just as I was about to walk Tara, Hunter, and Rufus, so at the moment we are all ambling through Eastside Park.

"Have they recovered?"

He nods. "Seems like it, for two reasons. It helped them that they own a lot of the land that their businesses are sitting on. But they also got a very healthy cash infusion."

"From where?"

"Hard to say. Hey, isn't that a new dog?" Sam points at Rufus.

"We've been walking for fifteen minutes and you just noticed?"

"All dogs look alike to me."

"That's Rufus; he belongs to our client."

"What happens to him if the client . . . you know . . ."

"We don't think negative thoughts, Sam. But you can be sure Rufus will be fine no matter what. How did the business problems affect Franklin's personal wealth?"

"Now that he's gone, we don't have to throw his wife a benefit, that's for sure. And the building blowing up didn't hurt him any, at least not cash-wise."

"What do you mean?"

"He had a personal art gallery on the sixth floor of the building. Twenty-one paintings were lost in all, and the insurance company wound up getting stuck for forty-four million dollars."

"The artwork was not owned by the company?"

"Yes and no. Everything Franklin did was through the company; since it was private, he could do what he wanted. I assume part of the reason is that if it was all in the company name, it would shield him from any potential liability for anything."

"So the loss of the artwork and the resulting insurance settlement was a financial plus for him?"

"Hard to say. Technically, his net worth wasn't increased because the art was actually appraised at that much. He could have sold it at any time."

"For the same money as the insurance company paid?"

Sam shrugs. "Again hard to say. Maybe more, maybe less. Art is really only worth what people will pay for it."

"Was there anything else of particular value in the building? Other than the seven people?"

"Doesn't seem to be. Obviously the company collected

a lot on the insurance, but they rebuilt the place, so they would not have profited from that." Then, "How long are these walks?"

"Why? You getting tired?"

"It's cold out here."

"That happens a lot in winter," I say. "We do a long walk, pretty much to the end of the park and back. They love it."

"Including Rufus?"

"Seems to. And the best part is he lets Tara set the pace. Tara doesn't like to be rushed."

"Rushing would be okay about now," Sam says.

"You can go back and curl up by the fireplace. But first tell me what else you learned."

"Not much else. I'm still working on it. I mean, there's a lot of personal stuff. Franklin had been married for ten years. It was his second marriage. Seems to have gotten hitched soon after college, but it only lasted a couple of years. He never had any kids."

"When did he start the company?"

"It sort of evolved. He was involved in a lot of this stuff, owning franchises in the various industries. But it was about eight years ago that he put it all under one roof, which was Marstan."

"Have they had any significant problems besides the COVID issues? Any major lawsuits, problems with regulatory agencies?"

"If they have, I haven't found any yet."

"They own jewelry stores, right?"

"Right."

"Where do they get their jewelry?"

"They import it, mostly from China and India."

We walk for a while and then Sam asks, "You think he could have blown up his building just to collect on insurance for the artwork?"

"I have no idea; it's one of the possibilities we'll look into."

"If he was trying to collect on the art, he could have blasted the place at any time, like three o'clock in the morning. Why do it then and kill all those people? Doesn't make sense."

"True. I need you to work on something else."

"If I do, can I go back to the fireplace?"

"Yes. I want Franklin's phone records for the two weeks before and after the explosion, and for the two weeks before his death."

"No problem, but I can only do his cell phone and home number, if he has a landline. Any outgoing calls from his company could have come from anyone in the office building."

"Understood. I also want a list of any cell phones that were in the area of his house when he was killed." Sam has the ability . . . I think it's by checking cell-tower records . . . to locate cell phones by their GPS.

It would be legal for him to do so, except that it violates the law. I'm willing to overlook that; I'm big that way.

"Will do," he says.

"Okay, you can head back to the fireplace."

"You know you don't have any wood in your fireplace, right?"

"So curl up by the stove."

"How many times a day do you do this? I mean, this walk."

"At least three. Depending on whether I'm home most of the day or not."

"What if it snows?"

"The dogs love the snow."

"What about you?"

"I love whatever the dogs love."

Echelon is a high-end auction house on Sixty-eighth Street and Madison Avenue in Manhattan.

I drive into the city and park in a lot on Sixty-fourth Street. For the cost of the parking, I could have taken a private plane here, but there is no place to land on Madison.

There also aren't that many places to shop in this area anymore; I am struck by the number of empty stores for rent, stores that used to contain pretentious merchandise that cost a ridiculous amount of money. Actually, the stores are more appealing to me empty.

I'm not sure if it's online shopping, or overly high rents, or a proliferation of people as cheap as I am, but these stores obviously could no longer make it work.

When I enter Echelon, I tell the receptionist in the lobby that I am here to see Wallace Linder, the managing director. "Yes, Mr. Linder is expecting you. He's in the auction room, and the session is almost over. Would you like to go in or wait here?"

"I'll go in."

She leads me to a room with two large wooden doors near the end of the lobby. We enter, and there is no mistaking that this is an auction room. Probably thirty people are present, with an auctioneer up front. I don't see any merchandise that he's auctioning off, but somehow that isn't stopping people from bidding.

Standing in the back of the room is a distinguished-looking man, probably in his sixties. He looks over at us, and the receptionist makes some gesture that causes him to nod his understanding.

She leads me over to him, and he shakes my hand. "Mr. Carpenter, welcome," he whispers. "This will be over shortly."

"Shortly" turns out to be twenty minutes, during which time a bunch of invisible items sell for a total of maybe $2 million. It finally concludes, and he tells me we can talk in his office. So I follow him there, which is up the steps to the second floor.

"What were they bidding on?" I ask when we're settled in. "I didn't see anything, or I would have been bidding like crazy myself."

He smiles. "Jewelry, from an estate collection. Extraordinary pieces."

"And these people were buying it sight unseen?"

He has sort of a condescending smile, and he uses it again. "No, the buyers had ample time in the viewing room beforehand. Plus, there were full appraisals attached to each. It was a remarkable collection."

"It seemed like there were some bids where I didn't see people raise their hand."

He nods. "There are clients who are connected online, and who see the room that way. They are already familiar with the pieces and can bid as if they are here. Of course, like those in the room, they have been approved financially before we begin the auction."

"Ever have anyone bounce a check?"

He smiles at the ridiculousness of the question. "Never." Then, "Do checks still exist?" He doesn't wait for an answer, just says, "I assume you want to talk about Stanley Franklin?"

"I do."

"A tragedy for the art world, a tragedy for our company, and a personal tragedy as well."

"You knew him well?"

"Certainly. He was very important to Echelon, and to me."

"How so?"

"He both provided and purchased many pieces. The finest works, often from some of the masters. And he shared my passion for those works."

"What do you mean *provided*?"

"Stanley was famous in the art world. People would come to him with pieces that they thought had value, and he was known to pay top dollar for them. Many of them came from overseas. If they were worthy, he would purchase them and bring them to us for sale. Often they were extremely valuable. If it was a piece that particularly struck Stanley, he might keep it for himself."

"So he had a valuable collection?"

"Extremely. Though some of them were lost in that horrible incident last year."

"Why did he keep those valuable paintings in his office? Do you know?"

"He told me that he enjoyed showing them to business associates and potential investors. He had a special climate-controlled room on a high floor, so they were well cared for."

"When he brought pieces to you to be auctioned off, he made money from this? You would buy them outright from him?"

"Certainly he made money; he was obviously entitled to. After all, he had paid for the pieces. But we did not buy them, we put them up for bidding. He would receive a portion of the purchase price when we sold them." Then, "I assume you know about the huge collection he uncovered that had been hidden since World War Two?"

"I read about it. Has it been sold yet?"

"No. We'll be soliciting bids within a few weeks."

"How much will it go for?"

"The minimum bid will be one hundred fifty million dollars."

"Must be nice paintings."

"Classics. They will draw far more than the one hundred fifty, but it's hard to say how much."

"The people who come here to spend those millions . . . do you validate their parking?"

As predicted, the call came in to Nick Edwards's cell phone every night, precisely at 8:00 P.M.

Each night he reported on Carpenter's movements, such as they were, that day. Carpenter did not seem to be doing anything of significance, but that wasn't up to Edwards to judge.

"He keeps walking those damn dogs," Edwards said on the latest phone call. "I follow him until he gets into the park and then wait for him when he comes out. The park is pretty empty these days, so he'd make me if I went in."

"That's fine," Sir said.

"Today he had someone with him. I confirmed it was his accountant; the guy has an office in the same dump as Carpenter. You sure this guy Carpenter is a problem?"

Sir didn't answer the question, just asked another one. "Did he meet with anyone today?"

"Yeah. I followed him into the city. He went into that auction house, Echelon. I couldn't go in there, so I don't know who he talked to."

"How long was he inside?"

"Forty-five minutes; maybe a little more."

"Then where did he go?"

"Back to Paterson, to walk those damn dogs again."

"We'll speak tomorrow."

"You want me to do anything about this guy? I mean, other than follow him?"

"When I change your assignment, you'll know about it. We'll speak tomorrow."

Click.

It annoyed Edwards to be spoken to like that, as if he were just an order taker. It furthered annoyed him that when there was something important to be done, Sir did not trust him to do it. Instead he became the driver for the man Sir trusted.

Edwards wouldn't say anything, of course, because he liked the money and because he had the feeling that Sir was not someone to mess with. Of course, Edwards was not someone to mess with either. He knew he could handle whatever came up.

Sir spoke with authority, and without doubt or hesitation. Edwards had no way to know if Sir was at the top of whatever totem pole there was, or if he was taking orders as well. And the truth was Edwards didn't much care.

As long as he was getting paid.

"Consider this an obligatory phone call," Joel Dietz says when I get on the line.

I haven't seen Dietz since the arraignment; he was confident then in the prosecution's case and there's no reason he shouldn't be confident now.

"Those are my favorite kinds, because we both want to get it over with," I say.

"Exactly."

"So let me get the ball rolling. You have a plea offer to propose, which would result in my client spending most or all of his natural life in prison. But you want him to turn it down because you mistakenly believe that you will win at trial and it will be great for your career."

He laughs. "You nailed it, except for the *mistakenly* part. Forty to life, all forty to be served before parole consideration."

"I think I can say with confidence that we will turn it down, but of course I will discuss it with my client."

"I understand. Shall we say that the offer is on the table until close of business tomorrow?"

"That seems reasonable. And just so we can avoid another

of these interminable conversations, if I don't get back to you, you can consider it a rejection."

Another laugh. "I look forward to not hearing from you."

"Let's not talk again soon," I say, and we hang up.

I head down to the jail to inform Jeff of the offer. I know he will turn it down, as he should. For one thing, it is not any better than he is likely to get after a conviction at trial, so there's no upside to taking it. For another, he swears he didn't commit the crime they are asking him to plead guilty to.

It's a good excuse for me to come down here anyway. I like to visit my clients regularly just so they will remember that someone cares about them and is fighting on their behalf.

It can get lonely for the client sitting in that cell, thinking that the system is running roughshod over him. Even if I have nothing particularly positive to say to them, like today, just my presence can be of some comfort. And it has the added benefit of getting me away from the incessant Christmas music in our house.

It doesn't take long for Jeff to turn down the deal, but I can tell that just thinking about it stuns him. He knows what he is facing . . . we've discussed it . . . but hearing that the state wants to put him away for forty years is jarring. And that they are asking him to accept it as a positive outcome compared to what might happen at trial has got to be scary as hell.

"I talked to Gerald Shuler," I say. "He agreed that you two didn't see eye to eye on how to deal with the aftermath of the explosion."

Jeff nods. "Right. We argued about it a lot. He was after the money, and in some ways I don't blame him for that. He couldn't get his wife back, just like I could never get Lisa back."

"And you weren't legally in line for any money."

"True. But what bothered me wasn't that. The fact that Lisa and I weren't married yet . . . we weren't even going to be engaged for a few weeks . . . it made them treat me like an outsider. As if my relationship with Lisa was somehow less important than everybody else's relationship with the person they lost.

"What irritated me about Shuler was that he didn't think I should even have a seat at the table because Lisa and I weren't family. That was hard for me to handle. But it was an emotional time for everyone."

"Is there anyone who shared your view that Franklin was responsible for what happened?"

Jeff thinks for a few moments. "I think so. There was one person, her name is Lillis; I think her first name is Kirsten. Her husband was Lisa's boss and he died that night as well. My sense was she was at least suspicious, but didn't want to come out and say it without proof."

"Good. I'll talk to her."

"Can I ask you a question?"

I nod. "Of course. Anything."

"Does it matter if I was right? I mean now, does it matter for my case?"

I have a smart client on my hands; it's a great question. "Not directly; whether you were right or not, the jury could still decide you killed him. It's not legal to kill anyone, even someone who blew up a building with seven people inside."

"That's what I was thinking."

"But we're trying to find out who actually murdered Franklin, and the best way to do that is to learn why they did it. And if you are right about his part in the explosion, then that's a piece of the puzzle. Because he had to have a reason to do that, and maybe he had accomplices in the process. It could all be related."

"Okay," Jeff says, his tone indicating he's not convinced.

"If it sounds like we're grasping at straws, it's because we are. That's the stage of the case that we are at. But we're also grasping for information; information is the coin of the realm."

"Okay," he says, still clearly not fully buying what I'm selling.

I take one more shot at it. "The worst thing we could do at this point is to formulate a theory and go looking for the facts to support it. It's tempting to do it, but if we're wrong, as we very likely would be, then we've accomplished nothing. What we have to do is assemble the facts, and the theory will organically come from them."

"You sound like you know what you're doing."

"Don't believe everything you hear."

I'm getting up to leave when he says, "I can't believe I'm going to be spending Christmas in this place. Tomorrow is going to be a depressing day."

That stops me dead in my tracks. "Tomorrow is Christmas?"

It's not my fault that I didn't realize tonight is Christmas Eve.

The odds were stacked against me because nothing in our house has changed to signify the arrival of the big day. The decorations and the music have been the same for almost two months, and it's not like we're throwing a party, or even going out. We stay home, just like we do almost every night.

I am blameless. It's a form of entrapment.

As soon as I get to my car, I call Laurie. "Why didn't you tell me tomorrow was Christmas?"

"I thought you'd figure it out, since tonight is Christmas Eve. The *eve* part usually gives it away."

"But how was I expected to know that tonight was Christmas Eve?"

"Uhh . . . because you live on this planet?" She seems disinclined to let me off the holiday hook.

"Okay, I will take partial responsibility for this, though I do so reluctantly. I rely on you to keep me informed about calendar issues. As you know, I've been engrossed in this case."

"I know that, and I am very impressed that you are

taking partial responsibility. It's a sign of how much you've grown."

"But there remains a problem."

"You did not buy gifts for Ricky and me."

"You have hit directly on the problem, and at this point, at five P.M. on what somehow, out of nowhere, turned out to be Christmas Eve, it seems insoluble. Unless you guys want a pizza for Christmas."

"The good news is I was able to anticipate this turn of events, mainly because it happens every year. I purchased gifts for Ricky and myself and charged them to you."

"Are you happy with what I got you?"

"Extremely. I have to say that your generosity blew me away, and your taste is improving. I'm sure that Ricky will feel the same way."

"Generosity and taste are what I'm about."

I head home, relieved that I've been absolved for my holiday sins, and I take the dogs for a walk. I didn't buy them anything either, but we have enough toys and biscuits that I think I can get by.

As you might have gathered by now, I'm not that big on the holidays, but I'm coming around. I've always loved the way Christmas lights look on the houses in the neighborhood, including ours. It somehow brings me back to my childhood, a happy time when I wasn't a lawyer.

Best of all is the way Christmas Day has turned into a televised-sports bonanza. The NBA has five excellent games on, spaced throughout the day. And the NFL has recently climbed on the holiday bandwagon with three games of its own.

It'll be me, Ricky, and the remote control, a perfect threesome.

We usually play a board game on Christmas Eve, the three of us. I suspect Ricky would rather be out with his friends, he's of that age, but he recognizes that family traditions are to be tolerated, if not honored.

Tonight we're playing Risk. Laurie doesn't feel Christmas is an appropriate time to be playing a war game with the goal of world domination, but it's Ricky's choice, so she's okay with it.

I'm the first one to exit the game, as I stupidly mass my troops in Norway and suffer a humiliating defeat by underestimating the Finnish military. I won't make that mistake again.

I watch the rest of the game from the sidelines as Laurie slowly but surely pounds Ricky into submission.

Nobody messes with Laurie during wartime, family or not.

For Christmas, I am going to give myself the gift of sports.

I am not going to think about the case at all. I am going to watch all eight NBA and NFL games without missing a single play, a feat that few people could pull off. But I believe I can do it because when it comes to sports-television watching, I have no peer. And when it comes to operating the remote control, I can humbly say that I am the Greatest of All Time, the Remote GOAT.

A murder case and trial is all-consuming, so this will be my last chance to get away from it. I'm not going to blow it. Televised sports will be the perfect gift, and it's a hell of a lot cheaper than what I must have given Laurie.

I take the dogs on a long morning walk, since later today our walk will be shortened to fit into a halftime. It's very cold today, but the dream Bing has of a white Christmas has once again gone unrealized. It's good that he's not around to not see it.

When I get home, I am surprised to see Sam Willis chomping down on pancakes that were meant for me. If he's embarrassed or contrite about it, he's hiding it well. His mouth is so full he can barely grunt "Hello."

He eventually finishes, after which Laurie tells me that she is out of batter, and that grocery stores are closed for the holiday. The day is not off to a great start.

"What are you doing here, Sam? I mean, other than inhaling my pancakes."

"Laurie didn't tell me they were yours."

I look at Laurie, who just shrugs. I'm not feeling a lot of repentance coming from her.

Sam continues, "I found out some information that I thought you'd want to know about right away."

"Does it have to do with the Detroit–Green Bay game?"

"No, it's about Stanley Franklin."

So much for a lawyering-free holiday. "What about him?"

"I checked his phone records for the couple of weeks before the explosion and before his death. There were a lot of calls to a lot of people I never heard of, so it's pretty much impossible to know what's meaningful and what isn't. I brought the lists."

"That's it?"

"No. There was one number that he called two days before the explosion. The same number called him back the next day. I thought it was unusual."

"Why?"

"Because it was an unregistered phone, commonly known as a burner phone. There is no way to know who owns it."

"So?"

"So it struck me as surprising that a guy like Franklin would be dealing with someone with a burner. Of course, there could be a lot of explanations, and it's not like Franklin had the phone himself. But then I checked the tower records of what phones were in the area of his house the night he was shot."

This is getting interesting . . . I may have to miss the kickoff.

"And that phone was there?" Laurie asks.

"Three blocks away."

"This may be worth giving up my pancakes for," I say. "Is there anything else?"

"Oh, yes; it's the reason I am bothering you on Christmas. I've located where the phone is now; it seems to belong to someone in an apartment building in Totowa."

"Any way to know who?"

"Not from the GPS. Could be anyone in the building."

"We can find out," I say. "We've done this before. We just follow the phone in real time when it leaves the building."

"There may even be an easier way."

"How's that?"

"You said that yesterday you went to that auction house, Echelon, on Sixty-eighth and Madison, right?"

"Right."

"Was it around two o'clock?"

"Yes."

"The phone was there too."

This just went from interesting to stunning, and the expression on Laurie's face shows she feels the same way. "In the auction house itself?" she asks.

Sam shakes his head. "Not necessarily, but if not, then

close by. And get this; he came here afterwards, at least to this street. Spent about ten minutes and then left."

I state the obvious: "He's following me."

"No doubt about it," Sam says.

"So we need to find out why, and who the hell he is."

Laurie nods. "I'll call Marcus."

The owner of the phone is Nick Edwards.

It was not hard to find him since he's been following me for days. Marcus has been watching him do it for the last two days, just in case Edwards is up to something more ominous than a surveillance mission.

Marcus got a photo of him and Laurie used her contacts at Paterson PD to identify him. Edwards is a hood who has been arrested on four different occasions, once for an unsuccessful jewelry robbery attempt, once for forging a check, and twice for simple assault.

He pled guilty twice, on the robbery and check charges, and has twice served more than a year in prison. He's not a Boy Scout, but nor is he Al Capone. Based on the reports Laurie has gotten from her connections, Edwards does not seem like a candidate for blowing up a building, or a brazen murder. But it's always possible.

Sam has been monitoring Edwards's phone, but unfortunately we haven't learned anything from it. I would have thought that he would be reporting to someone on my actions, maybe even daily, but the phone has not been used.

Marcus also said that Edwards has gone directly home

most nights, but went to a bar/restaurant for dinner twice. Marcus followed him inside and said that Edwards sat by himself and did not interact with anyone.

It's always possible, maybe even likely, that Edwards has used a different phone to report in, but of course we have no way to determine that.

Laurie, Marcus, and Corey are still trying to decide what to do about him; when it comes to a potentially dangerous situation like this, I cede total control to them.

But there is some tactical advantage to our knowing about him, without him realizing that we're onto him. At some point our need to get information will outweigh that advantage, but the timing of it is crucial.

We can't also completely discount the danger that the situation presents. While Edwards's phone was a few blocks from Franklin's house when the murder was committed, that does not mean with certainty that Edwards didn't pull the trigger.

With Marcus tracking Edwards while he is tracking me, it is unlikely Edwards could inflict any damage. Marcus is ready to intervene on a moment's notice if he senses a problem, and Marcus is an outstanding intervener. Marcus would lead an Olympic intervening team to a gold medal.

Criminals have become more conscious of the police's ability to track the GPS in phones. Edwards could have realized this and left his in the car, then walked to Franklin's house without it. Of course, if he was smart, he wouldn't have brought the phone with him in the first place.

Laurie's contacts told her that Edwards is an unlikely

candidate to be valedictorian at Harvard, which would seem to explain why he brought the phone with him at all.

In the meantime it's business as usual for me as I flounder around in search of a defense strategy. I'm on the way to a diner in Garfield to meet with Kirsten Lillis. Lillis's husband was one of the people killed in the explosion, and Jeff told me that he thought she shared his view of Franklin's culpability.

Lillis did not need any convincing to speak to me when I called her, which is always a good sign. Of course, there's always the chance that she chose a diner so she could throw hot coffee in my face. Such are the risks we lawyers face every day.

When I arrive, the woman at the reception stand directs me to a table near the back where Lillis is waiting for me. Next to the table is a fake fireplace and a fake Christmas tree. Remind me not to bring Laurie here.

Lillis smiles as I approach, always a good sign. She's already got a cup of coffee in front of her, and I order one as well.

I had told her in my phone call that I was representing Jeff, but she already knew that. "How is he doing?" she asks. "I always liked him."

"As well as can be. It's obviously a difficult situation."

"I'm not proud of something. When I heard that Franklin was killed . . . well, I didn't exactly break down in tears, you know?"

"You didn't like him," I say, proving that in any situation I am quite capable of stating the obvious.

"No, I never did. And I agreed with Jeff. I blamed him for Gary's death."

"What was Gary's role with the company?"

"He was a vice president in finance. He was there for four years."

"Why did you think Franklin was responsible for the explosion?"

"Gary was upset about something work related leading up to that day. He told me that they'd uncovered something about Franklin, that they sort of stumbled on it by accident, and that they were going to confront him."

It's exactly the same story that Lisa told Jeff leading up to that night.

Lillis continues, "Gary was worried about his reaction, which was why a group was going to be there together when they had the conversation. But they all recognized that they could lose their jobs as a result."

"But he didn't tell you what it was?"

"No."

"But you're sure this confrontational meeting was going to be that night?"

"Yes."

"It's a long way from that to killing all those people," I say.

"I know. But what got me, and Jeff felt the same way, is that Franklin denied that he was supposed to be there that night. I know for a fact that was a lie."

"You're positive about this?"

"I am, and I can prove it."

"Proof is always welcome."

"Gary told me a lot of this in an email the day he died. He was explaining why he was going to be late, and why he was upset about it."

"Can you get me a copy of that email?" I can always subpoena it, but I want Lillis on my side, and I definitely want her to testify at trial.

She says that she will and I give her my email address for her to forward it to me.

"Why would he lie about planning to be there unless he had something to hide?" she asks.

"I don't have the answer to that, at least not yet. Did Gary's group handle Franklin's personal business as well as the company's finances?"

She nods. "Yes. Gary wasn't happy about that; he felt it represented something of a conflict. He said that Franklin used the company's finances like they were his personal piggy bank. But since it was a private company, and since Franklin was paying for their time, he had the right to do it."

"If you don't mind my asking, did you get all the money you felt you were entitled to?"

"No. And I needed it; we have two children. Gary was thirty-eight; at that age you don't expect to . . ." She doesn't finish the sentence. She doesn't have to; the sadness on her face says it clearly.

"I'm sorry for what you've gone through."

"Thank you. Will you want me to testify at the trial? I can tell what I told you, and maybe be a character witness for Jeff?"

"I'm not sure yet, but I appreciate the offer. I will certainly call you if we need you." The truth is I will want her to testify if I can get the explosion to be relevant to our current case.

Other than that, she wouldn't be helpful. Unfortunately, she has no knowledge at all about Franklin's murder, and all she would do is reaffirm that Jeff and she shared a grudge against Franklin.

Also, that Franklin didn't pay the money that she and the other families thought they deserved makes her a biased witness.

What I would really need to know is what Gary and the other victims uncovered and were planning to confront Franklin with. But Lillis has no answer to that question.

Which leaves me nailed to square one.

Pamela Akers is a reporter who works for Vince Sanders.

It would seem that the main requirement for the position would be a high tolerance for belching and shirts with mustard stains. Amazingly, though, people who work for Vince say he's a great boss. One of them once told me that his staff would run through a wall for him.

Akers has agreed to come to my office for our meeting; she said she was going to be in the area anyway. Edna is not here, of course; I think she took the year off. Sam is down the hall doing whatever Sam does when he's not illegally hacking into stuff for me.

I try to do some quick cleanup, since I always leave the office a mess. But there is simply no way to make this place look like anything other than a dump, so I stop trying. If Akers works for Vince, she's used to slobs.

I hear her trudging up the steps from the fruit stand and I yell out that it's the first door on the left.

She enters, looks around. "This is your office?"

"Courtesy of my interior decorator."

"He or she has interesting taste."

She says she does not have a lot of time before another

appointment, so I get right to it. "You were working on a piece about Stanley Franklin?"

"Yes."

"Why him?"

"We thought he made for a compelling character. A self-made businessman, a renowned art collector, and a guy whose company had just had a devastating event . . . the explosion that killed seven of his employees."

"But you didn't write it?"

She shakes her head. "Unfortunately, no."

"Vince said Franklin complained about the way the piece was shaping up?"

"Yes. He somehow heard that it was not going to be the puff piece he was expecting, that we were going to ask some hard questions and maybe say some unflattering things."

"Was he right about that?" I ask.

"He sure was."

"What kind of unflattering things?"

"Mostly about his business. His company went through a very bad time during and after COVID. Not unusual because of the kind of things they owned, fast-food restaurants, mall stores . . . those kinds of things. At the time there were rumors that they'd go Chapter Eleven, or at least sell off a lot at basement prices."

"But they got outside investors?"

She nods. "Apparently of questionable character."

"Mob money?"

"Not so I could tell. It seemed to have been European, but I couldn't pin it down. The word, and I got this from sources within the company, was that these were the kind of people one didn't fool around with."

"Why didn't you run the piece?"

"Because we couldn't get reliable sources to go on the record. Vince, for all his faults, and he has many, is a top-flight journalist. You go with what you can prove."

"So it wasn't just because Franklin complained?"

"Absolutely not. That made Vince more anxious to run it. But we couldn't track it down, especially when our sources and information indicated that the money was from overseas. We're not exactly *Sixty Minutes*."

"Did you ever hear rumors that Franklin himself might have been behind the explosion?"

"As far as I know, the only person who publicly alleged that was your client. I never saw anything to support it."

"And I don't suppose you could give me the name of the person in the company who told you about the overseas investment?"

"Sorry. Confidential source."

"Can you put me in touch with the source? Maybe have them contact me? I'm really good at keeping confidences."

"Sorry . . . doesn't work that way."

"Then I won't tell you the name of my decorator."

"I can deal with that disappointment."

Not making good progress on a case is not a new experience for me.

Investigations don't always yield results, not right away and sometimes not ever. Secrets often don't reveal themselves, which is why they call them secrets.

But this case is unusual in one respect. For the most part, I haven't even been examining the crime my client has been charged with. I have been focusing on the explosion; it seems most likely to be fertile ground for concrete results.

But it may turn out to be an investigative non sequitur. It's entirely possible that, if successful, we'll uncover proof of a crime, or crimes, committed by Stanley Franklin. Then I'll be able to regale my client with the stories of it while he's serving a life term in prison.

The unfortunate truth is that at the moment we have no defense for Jeff Wheeler. He was at home at the time of the murder, but we can't prove that. There is incriminating evidence that we can't refute except to claim that it was planted.

Claiming a frame-up, with nothing to support it, has been tried three or four million times, and the next time it succeeds will be the first. So my focus has been on Stanley Franklin, to find out why someone would want to kill him, which could lead me to who did it.

Laurie and I have both called Margaret Franklin to try to arrange an interview to discuss her deceased husband. Not surprisingly, we've both been rebuffed. Margaret has not even come to the phone; the person that answered conveyed the message that we would not get to talk with her.

I tried the "We'll get a subpoena approach," but she was either unintimidated by it or smart enough to realize it was an empty threat.

I'm doing the next best thing today, which is to talk to a neighbor Corey found who claims to have been Margaret's closest friend, at least until recently. They became estranged in recent months, though Corey does not know why. Hopefully I can find that out for myself.

The former friend's name is Melinda Seeley. She lives about two winding blocks away from the Franklin home, and hers is almost as nice. I park in the driveway and from there I can see a pickleball court and a pool so large that two laps would exhaust Katie Ledecky. It's twenty degrees out, so I doubt that either are going to get used today.

I have no idea who named the sport pickleball, or why they chose that name, but one sure result is that I will never play it. I simply could not bring myself to tell anyone that I was pickling.

The sport itself seems to have little reason for being, an unnecessary compromise between Ping-Pong and tennis.

It's feels like a fad that's supposed to be hip, the racquet-sport equivalent of kale and pesto.

A man in shorts and a V-neck sweater answers the door. He's maybe five foot five and at least 230 pounds, none of it muscle. This guy has not spent much time either swimming or pickling, winter or summer. But he should definitely switch to kale.

"I'm here to see Melinda Seeley."

"You da lawyer?"

"I'm *a* lawyer. It would be presumptuous of me to refer to myself as *da* lawyer. I'm sure you understand."

He just looks at me as if I'm from Mars and yells out, "Melinda, da lawyer is here." Then, "Come on in."

The guy, who I assume is either Melinda's husband or her charm-school teacher, leaves the foyer just as Melinda appears. She's at least five inches taller and way slimmer than he is; if they played one-on-one basketball or pickleball, she would dominate him.

She walks over to me, hand extended and smiling. "Mr. Carpenter."

"Andy."

"Andy, then. I'm Melinda Seeley. We can sit in the den."

We head into the den and there is an elaborate spread of various kinds of cookies and muffins, along with some pitchers and cups. She definitely prepared for this meeting. "Are you a coffee or tea man? I'm guessing coffee."

"Good guess."

Before too long we're settled in and she's talking about her relationship with Margaret Franklin. "I mean, we were the best of friends, you know. We could read each other's minds. We finished each other's . . ."

"Sentences?"

"Right."

"But that changed?"

"I'm afraid so. I mean, it's not like we had a fight or anything. I still see her at the club and around and we're friendly, but it's different."

"Did the change predate her husband's murder?"

"Oh, yes. By a couple of months, or more. She just became distant and closed off; I mean, we used to share everything."

"And you don't know why?"

"No. I mean, I know she was having problems with Stanley."

"What kind of problems?"

"They hadn't gotten along in a very long time. I hate to speak badly of the dead, but Stanley was a charming, world-class asshole. He treated her like she was nothing."

"But she obviously stayed with him."

Melinda nods. "Yes, she did, although she kept telling me she'd had enough and she was bailing out. I know they had a prenup, and . . . I really shouldn't say any more."

"Of course you should. We're trying to solve a murder here." I know she's dying to tell me whatever it is she has to say, she just doesn't want to look like a gossip. Of course, she defines the word *gossip*; she could be wearing a sandwich board announcing that as her occupation.

"I guess you're right," she says, predictably. "I think Margaret found another outlet, if you know what I mean."

"She was having an affair?"

"You obviously know what I mean. I don't know who it was, or if it was even just one guy, but she hinted at it on more than one occasion. I think she felt bad about it, but not enough to stop."

"Did you know Stanley well?"

"I wouldn't say 'well,' but we spent time at the club. That was plenty. Stanley and his paintings . . . so pretentious. He talked about Renoir like they played pickleball together every Sunday."

"Margaret didn't share that interest?"

"Actually, she did. She knows more about it than he did. He liked the status, to be able to tell people that he had a Picasso, you know. She likes that part also, but she really understands it, certainly more than he did. I think she was an art major at Amherst, or Mount Holyoke . . . one of those."

"Did they have any financial problems?"

"Not that I know of; I really doubt that. I mean, Stanley spent fortunes on that artwork, and he sure bought Margaret expensive jewelry, that I can tell you. Then there's this whole Nazi thing, which will bring in a fortune."

"Nazi things are like that. Some of his art was destroyed in that explosion at his office. You don't think he could have done that for the insurance money?"

"I mean, you never know about people, but I can't see it. And Margaret would have left him for sure if she thought he'd done that. She loved those paintings, and she definitely loved to tell people that they owned them. Like I said, she was like Stanley in that regard."

Melinda tells me that as far as she knows, Stanley Franklin had no enemies. It's amazing how many murder victims I run into that did not have enemies.

I thank her and leave without seeing her husband again. I'm going to miss his wit.

I don't have a "suspect list," but if I did, Margaret Franklin would have just secured a place on it. If Melinda is correct, then Margaret and Stanley Franklin were having marital woes, and if not for the prenup, she might have left him.

Nothing makes a prenup disappear faster than a couple of bullets in the back.

Marcus decided it was time to make a move, and I was fine with it.

At a meeting with Laurie, Corey, and me, Marcus said that Edwards had started to follow me even more closely, at times being very near me. Apparently he is not worried about my catching on to him. And he is right about that; we're only aware of him because Sam traced his phone.

Edwards has been armed; Marcus could see the bulge in his jacket. There is always the chance that he could grab his gun and take a shot at me before Marcus could stop him.

I said that I didn't see any reason that would happen; it's not like we're closing in on the bad guys. But I can't discount the possibility entirely since I don't know why Edwards was tailing me in the first place. And when it comes to people who might kill me, I usually think it's best to assume the worst.

The call from Marcus comes at seven o'clock with instructions for us to meet him at the playground in Pennington Park. My guess is he chose that as the venue because it's near where Edwards lives. Marcus probably grabbed him as he was heading home after an unproductive day of following me.

We go in one car, and Corey brings his canine partner, Simon Garfunkel. It's been a while since Simon has chewed on a bad guy, and Corey thinks Simon will enjoy being back in the action.

It's cold and dark out, which is not all that unusual for nighttime in December in Paterson. I'm not nervous, which is unusual for me when headed into a contentious situation that does not take place in a courtroom.

I feel like Marcus, Corey, Laurie, and Simon are going to be more than enough to handle anything that Edwards might try to do. They could pretty much handle anything anyone might try to do.

Pennington Park was the scene of a number of my youthful baseball embarrassments. I struck out more there than I did at fraternity parties and bars in my college days.

We head for the playground, which is well into the park. No one else is around, which is to be expected, considering the time and temperature. A thin covering of snow is on the ground, which will be here in some form until April.

There is some moonlight, and in it we can see Marcus's car as we pull up. We get out and Simon immediately heads toward what passes as the merry-go-round. It's not like a carnival merry-go-round, it's just a large circular bench with spokes leading to a center. It spins around when people push it; it's high-tech, Paterson-style.

As we get close, we see Marcus, but not Edwards. Closer still, it turns out that Edwards is sitting down within the apparatus. Laurie takes out her phone, turns on the flashlight, and we can see that he has a rope around his neck and each of his ankles, all tied to a post.

If someone were to push the ride in the way it is meant to be pushed, Edwards would not fare well, to say the least.

"Happy New Year," I say when we reach him. "You have plans for New Year's Eve, or are you going to stay home and watch the ball drop? That's assuming you're still alive at that point."

He ignores that, which makes perfect sense. "You guys have to help me. Please."

"So you met Marcus Clark?"

"Yeah. And I've heard all about him. Please, call him off."

"No problem, we should be able to wrap this up quickly, as long as you answer a few questions. Let's start with, why have you been following me?"

"They told me to. It was just a job. I didn't do anything to you."

"Who told you to?"

"I can't say anything about that. I'd be a dead man."

"You think you'd be worse off than you are now? Seems hard to believe."

"I don't even know who the guy is; I just call him Sir. I talk to him on the phone, that's all. I swear."

I turn to Laurie. "He swears, so he must be telling the truth."

"I don't know," Laurie says. "Even though he swears, he might be hiding something. I've seen that happen."

Just then Edwards's phone rings.

"Answer it," I say. "On speakerphone."

He hesitates and I add, "Or Marcus can test how fast this thing rotates."

That idea apparently doesn't appeal to him, so he takes out his phone and puts it on speaker. "Hello."

"Where are you at this moment?" The caller's voice is distinctive—measured, precise, and calm, like a college professor's.

"Almost home."

"You were supposed to be there already, as we have discussed."

"I know. Sorry, I'm heading there now."

"You are not alone." It's a statement, not a question. The caller is stating a simple fact.

"No, I'm alone," Edwards says, the worry evident in his voice. "You want to know where Carpenter went today?"

Click.

"Shit," Edwards says. "He knows."

"No, he suspects," I say. "You can convince him. Tell him you went out for a beer with the guys and the time got away from you. What's his name?"

"I told you, I don't know. I call him Sir."

"You need to tell us everything. Believe me, Marcus is the greater danger right now."

"I can't."

"No problem," I say. Then, "Marcus, do whatever the hell you want with him. Enjoy yourself, but make sure no one finds the body parts."

"Hey, come on," Edwards pleads.

Laurie, Corey, Simon, and I head back to the car and drive away.

Marcus shows up at ten thirty, which means Laurie wins the pool.

I bet he'd be back before ten o'clock, and Corey thought it would be even faster than that. Marcus might be getting soft in his old age.

Most of the time, Marcus speaks in barely decipherable grunts, but for some reason Laurie understands him completely. Corey and I are not quite as good at it, and when Marcus debriefs us, I pick up about half of what he's saying. Once he leaves, Laurie fills in the gaps.

What was never in question is whether Edwards would tell Marcus everything. Marcus has a remarkable ability to get people to open up; he can be a real charmer when he puts his mind to it.

The bottom line is that Edwards really does not know the name of the person who called him while we were there, but he knows enough to be scared of him.

He has done a number of jobs for him over the years, some of which involved picking up special shipments at a pier in Newark, shipments that he believes successfully eluded customs.

One name that Edwards did know, and that he reluctantly

gave up, was Tony Bradley. He says he drove Bradley to Franklin's Alpine neighborhood the night of the killing and parked three blocks away.

Bradley got out and walked to Franklin's house. He was gone about a half hour. When he returned, Bradley told him that Franklin was dead, but that he didn't kill him. Edwards did not believe him, but had no reason to confront him about it.

Edwards also says that Bradley has a partner, but he doesn't know his name and has never seen him. Edwards believes the partner is even more intimidating and dangerous than Bradley, but he didn't tell Marcus why he believes that.

Edwards swears he himself did not kill Franklin, that he's not a murderer. He also told Marcus that he would testify in a trial, but he would have told Marcus anything to get out of his predicament. The chance of me getting Edwards to reveal all of this on the stand is absolute zero . . . maybe less.

Edwards said that he did not know why he was following me. He did what he was told and reported back on the 8:00 P.M. phone call every night where I had gone. He said he was never told to attack or hurt me in any way and wouldn't have done so if asked.

Not sure I believe that.

The most remarkable thing that Marcus has to report is that Edwards believes Tony Bradley and his partner were involved in blowing up the Marstan offices and killing those people. Edwards didn't say why he believed that, which means he might have been involved also.

If Edwards is smart, and I have no evidence to support that possibility, then he should now be spending his time concocting a story to tell the guy who called him on the phone. And if that story isn't ironclad great, then he should be packing to leave town.

The guy on the phone is clearly nobody's fool; he recognized immediately that something was wrong and disconnected the call. Edwards has to convince him that all was normal, which is going to be an uphill climb.

When the update is finished, I ask, "Does anyone know this Tony Bradley?"

"The name sounds familiar," Corey says, "but if Edwards wasn't lying, it shouldn't be too hard to find out who it is."

Edwards had two phones; one was probably dedicated to conversations with the guy who called him tonight. Marcus took both of them, correctly assuming that Sam might be able to get valuable information from them.

Of course, that will compound Edwards's problem. He is going to have to include in his story to his boss how he came to lose the phones. I have no idea how he will do that, but I'm not going to stress about it.

My guess, and that's all it is, is that Edwards will decide that he will never be able to convince the guy he calls Sir that he didn't rat them out. Once he comes to that decision, he'll go on the run, and we'll never see or hear from him again.

I will need some time to process all this. We got some good information, but nothing we can yet use in court.

So I'm pleased—at least I am until Laurie speaks up. "This puts you in more danger."

"Why?"

"Because unless Edwards can successfully lie to his bosses, and I doubt he'll be able to, they will know we are getting close to them. At that point, just keeping track of you may not be enough to ease their mind."

"Not sure I agree with that."

Laurie smiles sweetly. "Not sure if I care if you agree with that, honey. Marcus will stay with you."

I could argue the point, but I won't win and down deep I don't want to win. If not for Marcus, there would already be a memorial plaque with my face on it in the fruit stand under my office. Tourists would be told that Andy Carpenter ate his last peach at this very spot.

"Okay, so for now we look into Tony Bradley. He's the short-term key to this, and he's probably the shooter. I'll get these phones to Sam in the morning, and he can do what he can do."

"Oh, I forgot," Laurie said. "Marcus got him to give up the code to open both phones. He made him demonstrate it to make sure he was telling the truth."

Laurie hands me a piece of paper with the code written on it, and I'll give it to Sam in the morning.

"Good night's work, everyone," I say. "We pick it up again in the morning."

It isn't that often that I get surprised at a turn of events on a case. I've pretty much seen everything.

But I was surprised by a phone call this morning. Margaret Franklin, Stanley's widow, called and told me she had changed her mind. She would see me and answer my questions. That tonight is New Year's Eve did not seem to factor in her decision.

Well, she didn't actually call me herself. A man called on her behalf and said he was representing her. I'm not sure what he meant by that, but there's time to find that out later. In the meantime, I'm supposed to be at her house at 11:00 A.M.

That gives me time to have coffee with Laurie and take the dogs for a long walk. I was going to first bring the phones to Sam, but since I'm going to be rushed, I ask him to pick them up.

I was also going to ask Ricky to accompany me on the dog walk. He likes doing it, and it's a good chance for us to spend time together. But in light of last night's events, I don't want to expose him to any potential danger.

I don't know if Marcus is following me yet; Marcus is

only seen when he wants to be seen. I suspect that he is, but I can't worry about it.

I've been to the Franklin house before, but never went in. Laurie and I stood out front and assessed what was the murder scene, as well as the surrounding neighborhood.

I ring the bell and a man comes to the door dressed like he's about to leave for the senior prom. His dress and demeanor scream "butler."

"Good morning," he says.

"Let me guess. Jeeves."

He smiles. "Frederick."

"Damn, that was my next guess."

"You are Mr. Carpenter?"

"You got it on the first guess."

He steps out of the way so I can come in, which means I am standing in the spot where Stanley Franklin was killed. There is no plaque, and certainly are no bloodstains, to mark the spot.

"They will meet you in the den."

I note the pronoun *they* but don't ask any questions. Frederick doesn't seem like the talkative type, and I'm going to find out soon enough who *they* are.

He leads me to the den, where two people are waiting for me. One I'm sure must be Margaret Franklin; she can't be more than five feet tall but seems to be trying to look intimidating with a stern, unsmiling expression.

The other person is a man in his sixties wearing a suit and a fake smile. He stands to greet me and shakes my hand. Margaret offers her hand, but from a sitting position.

"Mr. Carpenter, my name is Randall Erskine. I'm with Erskine, Richards and Walters. Perhaps you've heard of our firm."

"Perhaps not."

"I am the attorney for the Franklin family. Mrs. Franklin has asked that I sit in on your meeting."

"That will be a treat."

He seems unfazed by my sarcasm. He sits down and says, "Let's begin, shall we?"

I start by saying that with their permission I am going to tape the conversation on my phone so that I don't have to take notes. I don't have to do this; I could do it secretly since New Jersey is a one-party-consent state.

But they don't object, so I start with "Mrs. Franklin, I'm sorry for your loss."

"Yet you are representing my husband's killer."

"Let's agree to disagree about that." Then, "How much knowledge did you have about your husband's financial interests, both business and personal?"

Erskine cuts in, "Mrs. Franklin will not be discussing personal details, certainly not about family finances."

I ignore him and turn back to her. "Was your husband worried about anything in the weeks leading to his death? Anything he shared with you?"

Erskine again: "Mr. Carpenter, I'm sure you understand that Mrs. Franklin will certainly not reveal private discussions between her husband and herself."

"Got it." I turn back to Franklin. "Do you have any favorite recipes you might share?"

"What kind of question is that?" Erskine asks.

I ignore him and speak to Franklin. "You agreed to talk to me, and I don't talk through third parties, even if they work at Erskine, Richards and Whatever. I have questions for you; you can answer them now or you can answer them on the witness stand. But this is wasting all of our time."

I start to stand and she says, "Understood. I agreed to this meeting because I wanted to get a sense of who you are and why you are representing this man. I also want to make sure that Stanley's murderer is correctly identified and punished. If there is the slightest chance that the wrong man is charged, and the real animal that did this gets away . . . well, that is an outcome too horrible to contemplate. So I'll answer your questions . . . within reason."

"Margaret . . ." Erskine starts, but she cuts him off.

"It's fine, Randall. Let's get this over with." Then, to me, "Stanley and I were open about our finances to a degree. He handled everything, and while nothing was a secret, I wasn't really involved day-to-day. I had no reason to be; he was quite capable."

I don't have anything to add yet, so she continues, "And he did not express any particular concerns in the weeks before he died. There were typical business worries, and issues with his art obsession, but nothing that seemed out of the ordinary.

"During that time he was very focused on the art treasures his investigators uncovered in Europe. Your client was becoming a minor annoyance, but I don't believe Stanley thought he represented a physical threat."

"Are you involved with the auction of those paintings?"

"Not really. Wally is handling that with Wilson Paul. They are quite capable."

By "Wally" I assume she means Wallace Linder, the managing director of Echelon. "Do you share what you call your husband's 'art obsession'?"

Erskine cuts in, "I really don't see how that has any relevance—"

"Perhaps you should take a night course in relevance detection," I say.

"It's fine, Randall. I did not, and do not, share it. I appreciate the paintings, at least some of them, but not to the level that Stanley did."

If anything, this makes me more suspicious of Margaret because this runs counter to what her friend Melinda Seeley told me. She said that Margaret was an art major who loved it and knew more about the field than her husband did.

But that's not what she's saying. She continues, "He tried to educate me, with limited success. And he certainly seemed to want our friends and associates to believe I was fully on board."

"Weren't you an art major in college?"

She smiles. "You do your homework. I minored in art, and I tried to get into it, but it never stuck. If you don't love it, I mean deeply in your soul, then it becomes an acquired taste and never truly takes hold of you. Do you understand what I'm saying?"

"Sure. It's the way I am with football."

I like to jump around when questioning potential witnesses; it can make them uncomfortable and less likely to repeat practiced answers. "I read your interview with the police; it said you did not hear shots fired."

"That's correct."

"Do you know how long it was from the time of the shooting until you discovered what happened?"

"A matter of seconds. I heard him say something like 'What are you doing here?,' but I didn't hear a response. Very shortly after that I went down to see what was happening and who was the visitor."

"So other than your husband's question, you heard no other conversation from either party?"

"Correct."

"And then you found him lying there and immediately called nine one one?"

"Yes. I was distraught. I'm not sure if I went to him first; I probably did."

"Does the name Nick Edwards mean anything to you?"

She thinks for a moment. "No. Nothing comes to mind."

"What about Tony Bradley?"

Another pause. "I don't think so. It sounds vaguely familiar, but I can't place it. And it's a common name."

"Your husband never mentioned either of these people?"

"Not that I can recall."

Erskine interrupts, "I think you've taken up enough of Mrs. Franklin's time."

I turn to him. "Thanks, you have been invaluable to the process. Whatever you bill for this will have been money well spent."

"Margaret . . ." he says, looking for support. I doubt he appreciates this Perry Mason wannabe, me, mocking him.

"Are we done, Mr. Carpenter? Do you have what you need?"

"I do. I appreciate your doing this. You have a lot on your plate, especially with the business."

She smiles sadly. "Where I grew up, we had a phrase, 'There's magic in every beginning.' I'm about to test that."

She calls to Frederick, who appears so quickly he must have been listening in outside the door. She asks him to show me out, and he does. We pass by a winding staircase. I'm not sure why some staircases wind and others don't; maybe there's a structural reason. This one is particularly long and winding; must be difficult to navigate.

"Is the master bedroom up there?" I point to the staircase.

"Yes."

"You have to go up and down that thing often?"

He smiles. "More than I'd like."

I shrug. "It's a job. You gotta do what you gotta do."

"Is that true of your job as well?"

"Unfortunately. We should both quit."

"Happy New Year," he says.

"Happy New Year, Frederick."

Laurie, Ricky, and I spent New Year's Eve as we always do, playing another board game and unsuccessfully trying to stay up to watch the ball drop.

I sometimes wonder how some of the things we earthlings do would look to alien visitors. Times Square on New Year's Eve is a good example. They would watch a million people gather in the freezing cold, doing absolutely nothing except pretending to be having fun.

Then a glass ball would slowly drop to the ground, which would seem to satisfy the lunatic earthlings, or maybe scare them off, because they would then quickly disperse. And then the aliens would no doubt move on to a different planet.

I know that soon, maybe next year, Ricky will insist on being with his friends on this night, and I dread that. So I cherish each boring New Year's Eve we all have together.

Nick Edwards had something of a less pleasant evening. His body was found by a couple out for a morning New Year's Day walk in Pennington Park.

I can't say that I'm shocked; I believe the guy on the phone, the one Edwards referred to as Sir, knew that Edwards was lying. Maybe he, or Tony Bradley or Bradley's partner, forced him to tell about his interaction with us.

I also can't say that I'm devastated by the news. Edwards was a thug. I don't know all the bad things he had done in his life, but by driving Bradley to Franklin's house that night, he was at the very least most likely an accomplice to a murder. If he was conscience-stricken about it, he hid it well.

It's not something that should have called for the death penalty, but Sir obviously operates a justice system more unforgiving than that of the State of New Jersey.

Of course, we directly caused Edwards's death by doing what we did, but I can't help that and I'm not terribly troubled by it. He should have understood what he was facing and taken steps to either protect himself or leave the area. We were doing our job; he was part of a criminal conspiracy that among other things commits murder.

The most interesting part of it is the location of the body. Marcus was clear that he drove Edwards to the park and drove him home afterward. So his killers, after learning what they could from him, took him back to the same park.

And there is no doubt that he told them what he knew. According to Corey's police contacts, he was beaten badly before being shot once in the back of the head. If Edwards talked to us that night, I am sure he spilled his guts to his killers.

They either killed him in the park or just dropped off his body. In either case, it was an obvious message to us that they knew what we were doing. It was also a clear threat and a challenge to show that they are not intimidated or worried about us.

I'm not thrilled with this, and not only because cold-blooded killers are threatening me. I had held out the faint hope that Edwards was smart and resourceful enough to have maintained his role in the group without having to reveal that he had talked to us. Then we could have gotten more information out of him down the road, an option that is now obviously closed.

I did not want Bradley to know that we were onto him, that we know he killed Franklin. That is now out the window, and it will make it more difficult to find out why he did it, and to prove it.

It also on some level increases the pressure on me and our team in the case. It proves beyond any doubt, at least in our mind, that Jeff Wheeler did not murder Stanley Franklin. It could not be that Edwards and Bradley happened to be near Franklin's house when he was murdered and yet had nothing to do with it. Coincidences that large simply don't exist.

So we've gone from believing and hoping Jeff is innocent to knowing it for a fact. That raises the ultimate fear of watching a client go to prison for a crime he did not commit.

But while we may know the truth, that is light-years away from getting the jury to believe it or even hear it. To get anywhere close to that, we must find out why Bradley and the people he works for wanted Franklin dead.

One thing is for sure . . . it had to be about money.

I believe they are the ones who helped finance Franklin

when his company was going south, and I further believe they were somehow profiting from their relationship with him. But then there came a time when he was more valuable to them dead than alive, so they made him dead.

Among the things we don't know is whether the explosion at the company building had anything to do with Franklin's ultimate murder. If it didn't, then it doesn't matter to us, and we've wasted a lot of time looking into it.

But we now have a pretty good reason to think it's connected. Edwards told Marcus that Bradley was involved in the building explosion. There is always the chance that he was throwing out nonsense to get Marcus not to kill him, but I tend to doubt it.

And if Bradley set off the explosion and also shot Franklin, then the conspiracy has to include both events. What we don't know is if the explosion was done with Franklin's blessing. It seems likely that it was, except that in the process they destroyed pieces of art that were precious to Franklin.

We won't know the truth until we know the facts.

And that may never happen; that's the scary part.

I spend New Year's morning with Ricky and our dogs at the Tara Foundation.

I don't come here nearly enough, especially when I'm in the middle of a case. But Willie Miller and his wife, Sondra, completely understand and let me off the hook. They run the place as a labor of love, and I appreciate their not making me feel guilty about leaving most of the work to them.

I don't have a lot of time; Corey and Laurie are waiting for me back at the house to discuss our current situation, and Marcus will join us as well. But I get great pleasure watching Ricky and our dogs playing with the dogs that are up for adoption.

Willie tells me that he's been reading about Jeff's case; he knew and liked Jeff from the Rufus adoption. "The guy that got killed, he's the one who found those paintings. . . ."

"What about it?"

"Those paintings are worth like a hundred and fifty mil?"

"Probably more than that."

Willie is clearly incredulous. "Just paintings, like regular paintings?"

I smile. "Yup. I imagine they're pretty good."

He is amazed. "For real?"

Something about his question strikes me, but I can't figure out why. "Willie, there's a whole world out there that you and I don't understand."

"And don't want to."

When we get back to the house, Corey, Sam, and Marcus are there with Laurie. Corey says, "None of the cops Laurie and I talked to have any personal knowledge of Tony Bradley, but we can be certain he is both a very dangerous individual and a piece of garbage."

"Why do you say that?" I ask.

"Because the reason that they don't know him is he's not from this area. He appears to originally be from Cincinnati, but he has arrest warrants out for him in Chicago and Vegas. One of them was for killing a cop."

"Does he have an ideology?"

Corey nods. "Money. He appears to work for the highest bidder, and it is believed that he does not come cheap."

"Do we have a photo of him?"

Laurie nods. "We do." She hands out copies to Corey, Sam, Marcus, and me. "You can't tell from the photo, but he's a big guy . . . six-two, two-thirty."

"Ever seen him, Marcus?" I ask.

Marcus shakes his head, all the while staring at the picture, probably memorizing the face for future reference. If I were Bradley, I would not want to run into Marcus. If I were Godzilla, I would not want to run into Marcus.

"Okay, so we know about Bradley, but we don't yet know who he is working for, or why they killed Franklin. Sam, what did you get from Edwards's phones?"

I don't bother mentioning that those phones may well have caused Edwards's death. He would have had a hell of a time explaining to his boss why he didn't have them. "I think I left them in a Starbucks" probably wouldn't have carried the day.

Sam says, "As you know, there were two phones. One of them was Edwards's regular phone, and there are quite a few calls on it. Most of them are innocuous, or at least appear to be, but a few of them may be of interest. I'll get back to that.

"The other phone was a burner and was used sporadically; there were periods of time where there were consistent calls coming in, and then weeks at a time of none at all. Calls were only received on this phone, never made. And in almost every case, the calls came in at eight P.M."

"Like the one the other night," I say. "Do we know who made those calls?"

Sam shakes his head. "No, and we're not likely to find out. They all came from four different numbers . . . they alternated. And all burners. They were from two different providers, one American and one German. And their GPS signals were disabled. There is no way to tell where those phones are, or where they were when they made those calls."

"So there is nothing actionable here?" Laurie asks.

"I'm getting to it. There is one thing that is unusual. Edwards's personal phone had calls to and from Stanley Franklin; that's how we found him in the first place. But there were also a number of calls to a Dierdre Millman.

"Two things about those calls are interesting. One is

that Stanley Franklin also called Ms. Millman a number of times. And the other is that Ms. Millman does not exist; there is no record of her at the address on the phone records, and no cyber record of her anywhere else. It's a fake name."

"So maybe Dierdre Millman is Tony Bradley?" I ask.

"Could be, but I can't answer that with any confidence."

"Is there a GPS active on that phone?"

"Yes and no. There is one, but the phone seems to be turned off when not in use. So it pops up, but not frequently."

"Can you tell where it was when it's popped up?"

"I'd have to go back and attempt that, but the answer is a qualified yes."

I ask Sam to do just that, and he leaves. Then I voice to the others a theory I am starting to lean to.

"We know Franklin and his company were bailed out of a bad financial situation by people that you don't want to piss off. So maybe the explosion was deliberately set to create a massive insurance payoff for the destroyed paintings, which would enable him to pay back at least some of the money."

"You want to go on, or should we jump in with problems?" Laurie asks.

"Jump in, the water's fine."

"Why would he have to blow up the building? Why not just sell the paintings?"

"It was a tough time; COVID had taken its toll. Maybe the paintings wouldn't have brought in as much in a sale as he got from insurance. Or maybe he didn't want to go public with his problems. He saw himself as a wealthy, big-time art collector, and now he's doing a fire sale? He wouldn't still be able to get a reservation for dinner at the Pompous Club."

"So he kills seven people?"

"Maybe that was unintentional. It was at night; usually the building is empty. And it's possible that his lenders destroyed the building without Franklin knowing it so he would get the insurance money to pay them."

"But you've heard that Franklin knew there was a meeting and that he was going to attend it," Corey says. "His then not showing up shows knowledge that it was dangerous to be in the building that night."

"Maybe he learned what was happening too late to stop things and save those people, and that artwork. Or maybe I don't know what the hell I'm talking about."

"All of this is possible," Laurie says. "Especially the last part."

"I'm not done. None of it was able to get him out from under the debt he owed, so they killed him."

"And destroyed any chance of getting paid?" Laurie asks.

"Okay, my theory may have a few flaws. So why are we sitting here? Go out and prove me wrong. Or better yet, prove me right."

Wilson Paul is really pissed off.

The way I can tell is that as soon as I get on the phone and say, "Hello," he says, "You are really pissing me off." I am excellent at picking up on subtle clues like that.

"Really?" I ask. "All I said was 'hello.' Should I have thrown in a 'good morning'?" I know why Franklin's minority partner is angry, but I seem to enjoy torturing him. I might benefit from therapy.

"You know damn well what I'm talking about. I was just notified that I'm on your witness list for the trial."

"Your testifying will be an act of civic responsibility. You should be proud, and you can invite your friends and family."

He seems not to be moved by that. "You think I'm going to say anything which could benefit your client?"

"I live in hope."

"Well, forget it, Carpenter. I will do everything I can to bury the son of a bitch."

"You sound like a hostile witness. Can't we all get along?" He's really starting to annoy me.

"You're damn right I'm hostile. What the hell do you want me to testify to?"

"I don't think I'm going to share that with you. I'm into surprises."

"Are you? Well, here's a surprise; I'm going to be your worst nightmare on that stand."

"I don't care what you say; just make sure it's the truth. There are laws about that."

"Your client killed my partner and friend and he's going to walk the plank for it. And I'm going to throw the first shovelful of dirt on him."

"You're mixing metaphors; you don't throw dirt on someone walking the plank. When he landed in the water, it would just wash off. Duhhh."

Click.

People seem to hang up on me a lot, to the point where I'm starting to wonder if there's something wrong with me. At the very least I must hang around with rude people. But it all works in the context of my not liking to talk on the phone.

I'm actually surprised that Paul was so angry about being on the witness list. The truth is that I was not even sure I would call him to testify; we lawyers always pad the list to give the opposition more work to do in preparation.

If I do call him, I'll ask him about the insurance settlement on the artwork destroyed in the explosion, and whether the company benefited from it. I'll also ask about the financial infusion that helped the company weather the downturn it experienced, and why no money has been paid back.

It wasn't a smart move by Paul to call me. He should

have known that his anger alone would not deter me from calling him as a witness at trial.

In fact, that anger makes me more likely to call him; it feels like he has something to hide. He probably doesn't; more likely he just doesn't want to be a defense witness, which comes with the implication that he is siding with Jeff.

But now I am sort of interested in what he has to say.

I would be in favor of jury selection by coin flip.

I understand it will never happen, but I am Andy Carpenter, rebel and visionary, and I think it would save time, money, and aggravation, without jeopardizing the rights of either the prosecution or defense.

I say this because the cold truth is that nobody knows what they're doing.

Lawyers agonize over each potential juror, doing psychological studies, hiring jury consultants, looking at jurors from every possible angle. Then, when the verdict is reached, we often realize that we were totally wrong in our pretrial assessments and would have done just as well with that coin flip.

I'm not going overboard on this. There should still be some challenges for cause when the situation is obvious. For example, if the defendant is African American, a potential juror should be dismissed if he shows up wearing a Klan hood. And a swastika tattooed on someone's forehead should also disqualify them, no matter who the defendant is.

I think the jury selection today in Jeff's case went well, or badly . . . I have no idea. We got an ethnically diverse group that pretty well represents Paterson, and none of them said they already thought Jeff should spend the afterlife burning in hell. Of course, maybe they thought it without saying it.

Who knows?

The gallery was full and the media were out in force. Franklin's prominence in the community, and that the auction for the stolen artwork is not that far off, guaranteed it. The auction is being talked about as the most significant event in the art world in decades, probably since paint by numbers was invented.

The day started with Judge Eddings predictably denying my motion for a delay. The media coverage of the auction is going to portray Franklin as a man whose last act before his death was to recover priceless artwork that the entire world can appreciate.

The jurors can't help but see some of it, despite what I am sure will be the judge's admonition to avoid all media. One thing I do not need is the jury admiring the victim.

So tomorrow these jurors will start listening to the State of New Jersey as it sets about the task of sending Jeff to prison for the rest of his life. They will listen with an open mind, or maybe not.

Who knows?

It's a coin flip.

"Ladies and gentlemen, let me start by thanking you for your service," Joel Dietz says to start his opening.

"Without juries we would have no justice system; they . . . you . . . are what allows it to function and, more importantly, keeps it fair. I know from voir dire and your questionnaires that most of you are serving on a jury for the first time.

"Well, let me tell you"—he smiles—"starting off with a murder case . . . that's jumping into the deep end of the pool. Compared to most cases, the crime at issue is more heinous and the potential punishment more severe. You will have to take on and handle that responsibility.

"But that doesn't mean your job is more difficult than other juries hearing other cases. You are deciding between the potential guilt or innocence of the accused, in this case Jeffrey Wheeler. Your task, the same as if you were deciding any other case, is to determine whether we have proven guilt beyond a reasonable doubt.

"And the way we ask you to make that determination is by following the evidence, pure and simple. Nothing I say, nothing that Mr. Carpenter says, is evidence. You should not take any of it as fact; you should only look at the evidence presented under oath.

"So what will that evidence show? Well, we believe that it will clearly demonstrate that Jeffrey Wheeler held a grudge against Stanley Franklin. And this wasn't your average, run-of-the-mill grudge. Not at all.

"Mr. Wheeler believed, without a shred of evidence, that Stanley Franklin, a respected member of the community, was a mass murderer. And one of his victims, in Mr. Wheeler's mind, was the woman he was planning to marry. So this was a serious grudge, perhaps a blinding one.

"And Mr. Wheeler did not keep the grudge a secret. He harassed Mr. Franklin and threatened him on more than one occasion. And when did the last threat come? In a public restaurant, one day before Mr. Franklin's death.

"But why did it suddenly turn violent? That is hard to tell; only the defendant knows that for sure. But we believe that it's because just before the murder, Mr. Franklin made a public announcement about his work in the field of fine art, one that won him worldwide praise. Mr. Wheeler couldn't handle that; he confided as much to people that he knew.

"You will also see and hear about forensic evidence, evidence so compelling that it will be proof beyond a reasonable doubt as to Mr. Wheeler's guilt.

"Let's be clear what we are talking about here. Someone walked up to the front door of Stanley Franklin's house and rang the bell. When he came to that door and opened it, the intruder raised his gun to fire. Mr. Franklin turned and tried to run and was shot twice in the back for his troubles. It was as cold-blooded as a murder can be.

"And none of what I have just told you is in dispute.

"If you believe with certainty that the man who came to that door, the man who raised his gun and fired, was Jeffrey Wheeler, then you must do your duty and see to it that he pays the price for his crime.

"But you must be certain, and that's the burden we, as the government, must bear. We must prove guilt beyond that reasonable-doubt line. It is the justice system's safeguard against unjust convictions and imprisonment.

"But the real safeguard for our society is you . . . the twelve of you. And all you have to do is your job.

"I know you will. Thank you."

As I look at the jurors' faces when Dietz finishes, they are either totally impressed with his delivery and what he had to say or bored out of their minds. There must be some secret juror training program that teaches them to look impassive. I know the judge never instructs them that way, but they all seem to do it instinctively.

Judge Eddings asks me if I want to give my opening statement now or wait until the start of the defense case. I always want to give it at this point; the jury is going to spend a lot of time being bombarded by the prosecution's case, and they need to have it planted in their heads that there is another side to the story. Our side.

"Ladies and gentlemen, I agree with Mr. Dietz that you have undertaken a very significant task, but believe it or not, at its core it is no different from what you have done pretty much every day of your lives.

"You have a choice. You weigh the facts and you make a decision. That's it. There's nothing new about that. The consequences of your decision may be more serious, maybe even momentous, but that should not be your focus. You should focus on the process and let logic be your guide.

"Jeffrey Wheeler did not commit this crime; he has never committed any crime, ever. Until this incident, he was never suspected, never arrested, never tried, and never convicted of anything.

"He owns his own business and is a combat veteran. He lost his girlfriend in a terrible explosion the night he bought the ring to propose to her. He performed heroically that night, but it was not enough.

"And, yes, he blamed Stanley Franklin for everything that happened. So, yes, he had a grudge against him. We stipulate to that.

"But if everyone who had a grudge against someone committed murder, the streets of this city would be a lot less crowded. The fact of the grudge is simply not strong enough to be evidence in a murder trial, not even close. The explosion happened a year ago, and Mr. Dietz would have you believe that after all that time, Mr. Wheeler decided to commit a murder?

"So what we are left with is circumstantial evidence; in fact, literally a bagful. None of it will make any sense, and we will demonstrate that.

"Stanley Franklin had enemies, enemies far more lethal than Jeff Wheeler. They are the ones that should be on trial here, and maybe, hopefully, someday they will be.

And then people like yourselves can make a decision about them.

"We will point them out to you and you will know exactly who and what I am talking about. And I believe you will have so much reasonable doubt about Jeff Wheeler's guilt that you will be bathing in it.

"And I also believe you will send him home to restart his life and end this nightmare. Thank you."

When I finish, I go back to the defense table. Jeff's face shows no emotion, which is as I instructed. The faces of the jurors are also just as blank as they were after Dietz finished because they are jurors and blank faces are obviously part of the job description.

"Great job, Andy," Jeff whispers when I finish. "The jurors were listening to every word."

"What else are they going to listen to?" Then, "The real action starts tomorrow."

"Mrs. Franklin wants to make sure this is done right, and she's asked me to get involved," Wilson Paul said.

He was meeting with Wallace Linder in the Echelon offices. Linder didn't want to take the meeting, but Margaret Franklin asked him to. She was the owner of Marstan Industries, and Marstan technically owned the paintings that were worth a fortune and were soon to be auctioned off. That made her one of the few people who could dictate his schedule.

"All of our auctions are done right," Linder said, slightly miffed at the idea that the firm would need help from Wilson Paul.

"I'm sure they are, but I don't care about the other ones. I care about this one."

"I am giving this one my personal attention."

"So how is it going to work?" Paul asked.

"It's already working. The pieces are in a private room upstairs available for appointment viewing by qualified buyers and/or their representatives. A number of showings have already taken place. An online presentation has also been prepared and sent to any potential buyers who request it."

"And the price is one fifty?"

Linder frowns slightly; it's a dismissive gesture. "As announced, the pieces will be sold together, and the minimum bid is one hundred fifty million dollars. That would represent an incredible bargain."

"What if no one meets the bid?"

"Based on discussions we have already had, that is not possible. I am hopeful of an enormous preemptive bid ending the evening early."

"How enormous?"

"That remains to be seen. I am not in the prediction business." What Linder did not tell Paul was that a bidder was already lined up, one that would be willing to go far higher than anyone else.

Linder would go through the motions and entertain bids from other major collectors, but none would go as high as the man that Linder already knew about. And then that auction would be an event that would be talked about around the world.

"So the auction will be held in the room downstairs?"

"In a manner of speaking. The pieces will be brought to the main auction room, where potential bidders and their representatives, as well as members of the media, will be present. We have already gotten far more media requests than we can accommodate. Our top auctioneer, Mark Chaikin, will handle it."

"Where will you be?"

"I will be next door. We own the adjacent building and

it's where our communications facilities are located. Many of the bids will come in electronically or by telephone. I will field them and convey them to Mark."

"How long do you expect it to take?"

Linder shrugs. "Once the bidding commences? Twenty minutes would be a long time. It could be far less. These are serious people; they know what they want and how much they are willing to pay for it."

"Who are they? I mean the ones you expect to bid the big money?"

"I'm afraid I can't share that; this is all done with the understanding of confidentiality, at least until the actual bidding begins." Then, "By the way, will you and Mrs. Franklin be here?"

"Mrs. Franklin wants to avoid the media and will be watching the live stream. I will be present in the room. How and when does the money get paid?"

Linder smiled. "I'm afraid I can only discuss that with Mrs. Franklin."

"As you know, this is being done through the business. I am a part owner of that business."

"Then you will soon be a rich man. But you will have to learn the financial particulars from Mrs. Franklin."

Paul was clearly annoyed. "You are aware there are other auction houses that could have handled this?"

Linder smiled. "Yes, I do know that. That's why I am especially grateful that Stanley chose us."

Dietz calls as his first witness Dr. Jacki Hagelberg, the chief medical examiner in Bergen County.

Dr. Hagelberg has been in her role for twenty-one years, and Dietz takes her through her career history to show that she has served with distinction. I'm not sure how medical examiners can serve without distinction, since their clients are already dead. How much damage can they do?

Dietz has called her to instruct the jury as to the cause of death. It's a real head-scratcher. Did Franklin die of the two bullets fired point-blank into his back, or did he develop a fatal case of the flu at the same moment, and the gunshot wounds were just a coincidence?

I could object, but "annoying waste of time" is not a legal objection. Besides, for Dietz it's not at all a waste of time. Hagelberg is there to give Dietz an excuse to show the photographs taken at the murder scene.

"There were two wounds which entered in the upper back and created exit wounds in the front," she says. "They entered approximately six inches apart."

"Was each sufficient to cause death?"

"Probably not. One went through the heart, inflicted

catastrophic damage, and was definitely the cause of death. The other missed internal organs and was likely survivable."

"Any way to tell which came first?" Dietz asks, for no reason that I can think of.

"No."

"Would death have been instantaneous?"

"Relatively so, from the heart wound. A matter of a few seconds."

"So he would have been dead before he hit the floor?"

"Yes, I would say so. There was probably still some brain function, but for all intents and purposes he was deceased."

Dietz introduces the photographs from the scene, which are quite bloody. They are designed to shock and horrify the jurors, and I suspect they accomplish that purpose.

Dietz asks if Hagelberg can tell the distance the shots were fired from, and she replies, "Maybe six feet. It's hard to be precise, but certainly not much further than that. Eight feet at the outside."

Dietz turns the witness over to me. There is obviously little for me to get from her; she has played the role of Captain Obvious in her testimony.

"Dr. Hagelberg, can you tell the jury who fired those shots?"

"No, I cannot."

"Can you tell the jury why Mr. Franklin was killed?"

"No, I cannot."

"So basically you are here to say that the man who received two gunshot wounds in his back, and then died with seconds, died from gunshot wounds in his back?"

"Yes."

"Did that surprise you? Were you expecting to uncover a different cause of death?"

"No to both questions."

"Was it your idea to show the jury the bloody photos?"

"No." She says that quickly before Dietz can object. When he does, the judge overrules it, surprising me.

"Was there any point that you made in your testimony that you needed the photos to demonstrate?"

"No."

"Do you think the jury and anyone else viewing these photos would find them unpleasant?"

"It would not surprise me, but I can't speak for others."

Eddie Dowd, per the plan, puts up on the screen a photo of Rufus as an adorable golden puppy, taken last year.

"Do you know what that is?" I ask Hagelberg.

"A cute puppy . . . maybe a golden retriever?" she says, before Dietz can jump up to object.

"Your Honor. This photo has not been introduced into evidence and has nothing to do with our case."

The judge turns to me. "Mr. Carpenter?"

"I'm sorry, Your Honor. I just thought that since the jury was being shown unpleasant photos for no reason, I should show a pleasant one for no reason." Out of the corner of my eye I can see some of the jurors smiling.

"Mr. Carpenter, I will not have these type of stunts and actions in my courtroom. Do you understand?"

"Yes, Your Honor. My apologies to the court." I then turn to the witness. "Thank you. No further questions."

When I get back to the defense table, Jeff is smiling. I

think he liked the exchange, but I really think he enjoyed seeing the photo of Rufus.

I assume the jury understood the implication of my questions about the photos. I further assume they realize that I am telling them that their emotions were being manipulated by Dietz, and I hope they resent that.

If they missed all of that, we do not have a very bright group deciding Jeff's fate.

It's not that I think any of this will determine conviction or acquittal. This was just a setup, and the next witness will be more of the same.

That next witness is Sergeant Peter Wilhelm of the Alpine Police Department. He was one of four officers to respond to the scene of the murder that night, and Dietz apparently decided that Wilhelm, as the ranking officer among them, should be the one to testify.

It immediately becomes obvious that the choice of witness was about more than rank. Wilhelm has been at this for twenty-two years and conveys a veteran's wisdom and unflappability that plays well with the jury. He also seems likable, with a quick smile and a nice way about him.

I'd be fine having a beer with him at Charlie's, but I'm not thrilled with his being on the opposite side of our case.

Dietz starts off slow. "Sergeant Wilhelm, you were the first to arrive at the Franklin house that night?"

"The killer got there first."

Dietz nods. "Point taken. I stand corrected, so I'll rephrase. You were the first member of law enforcement to arrive at the Franklin house that night?"

"Along with three other officers, yes."

"What brought you there?"

"A nine-one-one call from Mrs. Franklin."

With Judge Eddings's permission, Dietz plays the call. Margaret Franklin sounds distraught during the call, nearly hysterical. It is the audio version of showing the bloody photos, in that it is designed to horrify the jury and turn them against the defendant, since they have no one else to blame.

"What did you find when you got there?"

"The door was open, and the deceased, Mr. Franklin, was lying on the floor. Mrs. Franklin was standing in a corner of the foyer. She was crying."

"What did you do first?"

"I felt for a pulse and determined that the victim was, in fact, deceased."

"And after that?"

"I sent two of the other officers to search the rest of the house, to confirm that the perpetrator was not still present."

"Did they confirm that?"

"Yes. There were no people in the house other than Mrs. Franklin."

"Does this accurately reflect what you saw on your arrival?" Dietz asks, showing the photographs on the screen again. I frown, hoping the jurors will notice that I am disdainful of this obvious and repeat manipulation. A few of them look my way, so I'll take that as a small victory.

Wilhelm nods. "Yes, it does."

"What did you do after that?"

"We called in Homicide and the coroner and secured the crime scene. I then escorted Mrs. Franklin into the den."

"Did you question her?"

"Only to ask if she knew who the perpetrator was and if she knew his or her location. She answered both questions in the negative. After that I stayed with her until the homicide detectives arrived, and they took over."

My turn.

"Sergeant Wilhelm, it's my turn to show another photograph; this one without any blood in it."

Dietz objects and this time Judge Eddings sustains it, with an admonition to be careful. "Very careful" is how she puts it.

I show an overhead photograph of the entire Franklin estate, which was helpfully in the discovery materials. "Sergeant, this is the Franklin house and property, correct?"

"Certainly looks like it. And it's identified as a police photograph, so I would tend to believe that."

"Good. Here's a pool with a cabana house, right?"

"Yes."

"And here's a tennis court, and what is this?"

"Looks like another pool house, but I'm not sure. Maybe a guest apartment, maybe not. I just don't know."

"And you see all this shrubbery and trees on the outskirts of the property?"

"Yes."

"You said you had people search the premises to make sure the perpetrator wasn't present."

"Yes."

"Did you search these other structures? Did you search into the shrubbery and trees?"

"Not initially, no. That was done later when more officers arrived and Homicide controlled the scene."

"So it's possible someone was present somewhere in there initially and you would not have known it?"

"Mrs. Franklin told me that no one else was present. We confirmed that with the search of the house. We were limited in personnel when we first arrived."

"When did she tell you that no one else was present? You testified that the only conversation you had with her was to ask her if she knew who did it, and where that person was."

"I should have mentioned that I also asked her if she knew if anyone else was present."

"Yes, you should have. Is there anything else you left out that you should have mentioned?"

"No."

"No further questions."

I had nothing important to accomplish with my implying that someone could have been hiding on the property. That person could just as easily have been Jeff as anyone else.

My point was to show shoddy police work and hope therefore to call into question other things they did, and other things they discovered, later on in the trial.

It won't work, but I had nothing else to throw at Sergeant Wilhelm. There unfortunately aren't a lot of bullets in the defense gun.

I head home. My plan is to walk the dogs and then spend the rest of the night once again going through the discovery while dreading the rest of the trial.

Should be a fun night.

The first prosecution witness this morning is Gerald Shuler.

Shuler's wife, Cassie, died in the explosion at Marstan, and when I interviewed him, he told me he disagreed with Jeff on the approach to take afterward.

Dietz quickly establishes that Shuler owns Pirelli's Restaurant and that he has two children, aged fourteen and eleven. "My wife passed away," he says.

"I'm sorry for your loss. How did she die?"

"She worked for Marstan Industries. More than a year ago there was an explosion caused by a gas leak, and she was one of seven people who lost their lives. I . . . my kids and I . . . we miss her every day."

"Do you know the defendant, Jeffrey Wheeler?"

"Yes."

"How did you come to know him?"

"After it happened, the families of the victims . . . we got together and formed sort of a committee. We wanted to be compensated for our loss. I know that sounds cold, but there was nothing else we could do. Nothing could bring Cassie back, nothing could bring any of them back. So we wanted someone, anyone, to pay for what happened."

"Mr. Wheeler was a part of that committee?"

"Yes and no. He tried to be. But there were two problems with that."

"What were those problems?"

"Well, for one thing, he and Lisa . . . that's Lisa Dozier . . . they weren't married. In fact they weren't engaged yet. That doesn't mean he didn't love her; it was obvious that he did. But as a boyfriend, he was not legally entitled to receive money from the insurance or anyone else, so his situation was different than all of ours. The lawyer referred to it as not having legal standing."

"And the other problem?"

"Jeffrey thought that the explosion was intentional, that Stanley Franklin deliberately set out to kill all those people. He did not present any evidence for that, and we never saw any."

"So he told you that he believed Stanley Franklin murdered Lisa Dozier, and your wife, and the others?"

"Oh, yes. He told that to all of us, repeatedly. He wouldn't let it go, and it was interfering with what we were trying to do."

"So what did you do about it?"

"We told him that he should pursue whatever he was going to pursue separately from us."

"How did he react?"

"I think he understood, even though he wasn't happy about it. His anger was not directed at us, at least it didn't seem like it. He was angry at Stanley Franklin."

"He told you that?"

"Many times."

Dietz turns Shuler over to me; there isn't much I am going to be able to do with him.

"Mr. Shuler, you said you and the other families were trying to be fairly compensated for your losses."

"We could never be compensated enough."

"I understand. How did it wind up?"

"What do you mean?"

"Well, did you get the money you felt you were entitled to?"

"No, the insurance company found no negligence, they determined that it was an unavoidable accident. They paid, but not nearly what we felt we deserved. I do well, I don't need the money, but some of the other families were more in need."

"At any point, did you turn to Stanley Franklin? Since it was his company and his building, did you feel he should have contributed to the compensation as well? Above and beyond what the insurance company offered?"

"Yes, we did. But he rebuffed us . . . through his attorney."

I nod. "So he wouldn't talk to you personally?"

"No."

"Did that make you and members of your committee angry?"

"Yes."

"Did you kill him?"

"No."

"You sure? This is your chance to confess."

Shuler is annoyed; he's one of many people who do not fully appreciate my sarcasm. "I did not kill him."

"Did one of the other angry members of your committee kill him?"

"No."

"So they all had alibis for that night?"

Dietz objects and I withdraw the question. I try another one. "So it was possible to be angry at Stanley Franklin over a tragic incident and not kill him?"

Dietz objects again, the judge sustains, and I let Shuler off the stand.

During the break I check my phone and there's a message from Laurie. "Andy, we got a break. We may have found Tony Bradley. Everyone will be at the house tonight to talk about it."

That is the best news I've heard so far today, and nothing is in second place.

The next prosecution witness is Jerry Cawley.

We were just notified this morning that Cawley was going to be called; he's currently in the same jail as Jeff. I objected that he wasn't on the witness list, but Dietz said Cawley had just come forward last night with relevant information.

Judge Eddings had no choice but to allow him to testify, with the proviso that I could have a brief continuance afterward to prepare a cross-examination if I needed it.

I won't need it.

When Cawley goes to the stand, I ask Jeff if he knows him.

He nods. "Yeah, he's a guy in the jail. I see him sometimes when we get exercise time."

"Have you talked to him?"

"Once or twice . . . nothing important."

"Ever talk about this case?"

He shakes his head. "Never. You told me not to talk to anyone."

"Mr. Cawley, you are currently in the county jail, awaiting trial on an assault charge?" Dietz asks, to start the bullshit ball rolling.

"Right. A guy punched me and I punched him back. I punched harder, so I'm the one they arrested. It was self-defense."

"Mr. Cawley, did you come forward last night with some information relevant to this case?"

"Yeah. Yes."

"How did that come about?"

"Well, we have two hours of exercise time every day, in this area where there's a basketball court, weights, that kind of stuff. And I see him, Wheeler, there all the time. We talk about stuff."

"What kind of stuff?"

"Everything. You name it."

"So what is the information you have that relates to this case?"

"Well, one day last week he starts talking about his case, about this guy Franklin. I asked if he killed him, expecting him to say no, you know? Because nobody ever wants to cop to anything. That's just the way it usually is in there."

"What did he say?"

"That he did it. He said he went to his house and shot him. I asked if he was kidding, but he said no. It was like he was proud of it."

Dietz pauses a moment to let it sink in. "Did he say why?"

Cawley nods. "Yeah, he said that Franklin killed his girlfriend. They were gonna get married. Then he saw him on television talking about some art thing where he was gonna make like a hundred million dollars.

"It drove him nuts; he said there was no way the guy could get away with that. He said at first he was just going to scare him, but then he saw him and he just lost it, you know?"

"Mr. Cawley, did anyone from my office offer you anything in return for your testimony today?"

"No. I don't need anything. I'm not gonna go down for the assault rap. The other guy hit me first. I've got witnesses."

"Why did you come forward?"

"Because he was talking about straight-out murder. I'm not a Boy Scout, you know? But that's too much; that ain't right. I thought about it for a while and decided I needed to tell someone about it."

"Thank you."

I just about jump out of my chair to question Cawley. "Mr. Cawley, do people confide in you a lot?"

He shrugs. "Some, I guess. I'm a friendly kind of guy."

"I assume the person you assaulted would disagree with that?"

Dietz objects and Eddings sustains.

"Is this the first time you've been arrested?" I ask.

"A couple of other times."

"Spend any time in jail? I mean, besides your current situation."

"Yeah, twice."

"So you and Mr. Wheeler talked a lot?"

"Yeah."

"You became buddies?"

"Yeah, I guess. I mean, not real close or anything."

"So your buddy . . . the one you're accusing of murder . . . did he say anything other than admitting to that murder?"

"Sure. A lot of stuff."

"Like what?"

"You know, about how he felt about things. What he'd do when he got out. A bunch of stuff."

"Did he talk about his career?"

"I don't think so."

"About his wife and kids?"

"He mentioned them a couple of times, but didn't say too much."

"Did he say his son was applying to colleges?"

"I think he mentioned that, yeah."

"Your Honor, let the record show that Mr. Wheeler has never been married or had children. I can lay the foundation for that if it's necessary."

"Proceed for now," Eddings says.

Cawley speaks without being asked a question, trying to do damage control. "Maybe he didn't say anything about them. I don't remember."

"Can you think of one thing he said about his life in all your conversations, other than that he was a cold-blooded murderer?"

"I don't remember."

"Did anyone offer you anything in return for your coming here and committing perjury today?"

"Hey, I'm telling the truth. What's going on?"

Dietz jumps to his feet. "Your Honor, I resent the implication in Mr. Carpenter's question. I can categorically state that Mr. Cawley was not offered anything in return for his testimony. He came forward on his own."

"Your Honor, I want to be very clear about this," I say. "I do not believe that Mr. Dietz or anyone associated with him made any kind of offer to this witness. I one hundred percent reject that possibility.

"But that does not mean that Mr. Cawley was not offered anything. Someone clearly coerced him into lying."

"I'm not lying. I swear on my kids' lives."

"Mr. Cawley, don't say that. If you have kids, they've suffered enough."

"Marcus found someone who knows where Tony Bradley is staying," Laurie says.

Marcus is not here, but Corey has come to the house. Laurie is telling us what Marcus reported to her.

"How did he do that?" I ask.

"By working the streets and by being Marcus."

I tend not to focus too much on Marcus's methods; the less we know the better. Laurie and Corey have slowly bought into that approach as well.

"The guy's name is Charlie Silver, though Marcus doubts that's his real name. Marcus figures the guy has used so many aliases that by this point he may not even know what his real name is. But for now, and for our purposes, he's Charlie Silver."

"How does Charlie know Tony Bradley?" I ask.

"It seems that Charlie has a number of technical skills, including the ability to create explosive devices. Bradley had been looking for someone with that particular skill, and he found Charlie."

"So he wanted Charlie to make him a bomb?" Corey asks.

"Actually, no. He wanted a detonator to attach to an

existing device, which could be activated by a cell phone call. He offered Charlie fifty thousand dollars, which Charlie apparently considered more than fair, since it was well within Charlie's skill set and would not take much time at all."

"Did Charlie make it for him?"

Laurie nods. "He did, and he provided it to Bradley. Unfortunately for Charlie, and hopefully fortunately for us, Bradley only paid him twenty-five grand."

"How did Charlie react to that?" I ask.

"He complained of course, and Bradley mentioned that if Charlie was not satisfied with the twenty-five, he could arrange for Charlie to be dead. Charlie did not press the issue because Bradley is apparently a scary individual who did not seem the type to make empty threats."

"Why did he tell Marcus all this?"

Everybody looks at me like I'm nuts.

"Because it turns out that Marcus is also a very scary individual," Laurie says. "I thought you knew that."

I shrug. "I forgot."

"Anyway, Charlie had followed Bradley to where he was staying, apparently to be able to extract some kind of revenge down the road, without endangering himself. That's where Marcus came in."

"But Charlie did not know what the explosive was going to be used for?"

"He said he did not."

"So what is our plan?" I ask, knowing that Laurie and Marcus would already have come up with one.

"Marcus is determining whether Bradley is home. If he is, we head there now. He's staying in Ridgewood."

"So we're doing this tonight?" I cringe slightly. I'm always fine putting off anything that involves any kind of danger.

"Why not?" Corey asks.

Since I don't have a good answer, I don't respond. I have no way out of this if it's tonight. Ricky is in his room doing homework. I would say I need to stay behind to babysit him, but he's sixteen, so I can't get away with that line anymore.

Damn kids grow up so fast.

We don't have to wait long. Marcus calls, Laurie answers, and Bradley must be there, because we're on our way.

We meet Marcus at a 7-Eleven about a half mile from Bradley's house.

Marcus discusses the situation with Laurie and Corey, and they finalize their plan. I overhear it, but am not invited to participate in the strategizing. That's fine with me.

The house is in an upscale neighborhood, on a cul-de-sac. It has neighboring homes, but they're at least fifty yards away on each side. It can be approached from a street behind the house by going through about thirty feet of woods.

There is a lot of shrubbery along each side of the house, perfect for concealing invading humans. To make things even easier, no outside lights are on.

We park our car on that rear street. Corey goes around to the front of the house, while Marcus, Laurie, and I stay in the back. Marcus will approach the house by himself; the prevailing view is that one person will be less likely to attract attention. It's quite dark, so it's not difficult for Laurie and me to stay in the shadows and shrubbery and remain unseen.

Laurie will guard the back door and Corey the front,

in case Bradley is able to make a break for it. I will stand with Laurie; I guess my value in being here is that I could file a motion, sue someone, or perform some other lawyerly function. Otherwise I am to stay out of it.

Marcus heads toward the house. It's a little hard for us to visually track him in the darkness, and Marcus is dressed in dark clothing. He then walks to the left, still along the house. I assume he is looking in the windows. It's starting to rain, which is not a problem because I'm pretty sure Marcus is impervious to the elements.

We lose track of him as he walks around toward the front. He's probably gone from our sight for three or four minutes, but it seems like three or four months.

Suddenly we see him again, coming back around from the other side toward the back. He moves toward the back door, slowly and quietly. He may be testing it to see if it's unlocked, but I can't tell that in the darkness.

Then, so suddenly that I think I missed it, there is no door there anymore. Bright light comes through the area where the door used to be, and Marcus is silhouetted by it. The noise from the crashing door reverberates in the otherwise still night air. I can't speak for Laurie, but I find it stunning.

Laurie moves toward the house, gun drawn, waiting for the possibility that Bradley may come running out. There is no doubt that Corey would have heard the crash; I'm sure Ricky heard it back in Paterson.

Per the plan, Corey would now be moving toward the front door as Laurie is toward the back.

After just a minute or so, I hear a text go off on Laurie's

phone. She looks at it and says, "Marcus." I know that; also per the plan, Corey received the same text. It's a signal to come into the house, that Marcus has things under control.

We walk quickly toward the back door, Laurie more quickly than me. We enter, and about fifteen feet into the corridor we see Marcus. A large body is lying at his feet; I'm guessing, and totally hoping, that it's Bradley.

If this is just an innocent suburban homeowner, interrupted while watching *Real Housewives of Paterson*, we have a bit of a problem.

"Uh-oh," Laurie says, maybe thinking what I'm thinking.

But it turns out she's not concerned with who he is; she is worried whether he has gone to that great prison in the sky. She walks over to him and puts her hand on the side of his neck. "He's alive," she says with obvious relief.

"That's good," Corey says, having just arrived through the front door. "But he looks like he will be out for a while."

"We need to get information from him before we call the cops," I say. "So I guess we just wait."

The words are barely out of my mouth when we hear sirens; neighbors must have heard the door crashing and called the cops. Within moments two officers are in the house, guns drawn.

They look at Bradley's prone body and then us, and mercifully one of the cops says, "Corey?"

"Hey, Billy," Corey says. "What's new?"

"What the hell is going on, Corey? Who is that guy?

Who are these people?" The good news is recognizing Corey gets them to put away their guns.

"These are my friends and colleagues." Corey points to Bradley. "And this, Billy, is your lucky day."

"What does that mean?"

Corey points to Bradley. "This piece of garbage is wanted for murder in Chicago and Vegas; he's a cop killer. And you just captured him."

"You want to explain what happened?"

"Sure. We heard he might be here, so we knocked on the door to talk to him. He attacked us, and we took defensive measures."

"How did the back door get crashed in?"

"Must have been the wind."

"Corey, come on. This is serious."

"Billy, this is the biggest bust in this jurisdiction in decades, and we're dropping it in your lap. We're the good guys here. You figure out the story, okay?"

Billy looks at his fellow cop, who nods slightly. "Okay," Billy says. "Get the hell out of here." Then, "What's his name again?"

"Tony Bradley."

We turn to leave, but before I do, I tell Billy to make sure he finds and confiscates Bradley's phone. I'm sure they would do so anyway. When he calls for backup, which he'll do as soon as they figure out a credible story, they'll conduct a thorough search of the premises. But it can't hurt to mention it.

I notice that Laurie has not been with us in the corridor; I hadn't seen her leave. Corey, Marcus, and I go outside;

we wait for her, and a few long minutes later she comes out.

"No explosive device that I can find," she says.

"That's not good," I say. "Not good at all."

Dietz has an advantage over me today.

He had a chance to get a lot of sleep last night; he wasn't out invading a murderer's house and searching for a bomb. He could have had a pleasant dinner, spent a few hours preparing for his witnesses, and then turned in for the night, so he'd be fresh in the morning.

That's the kind of lawyer I want to be when I grow up.

Except that a killer was knocked unconscious and then taken into custody by police to face either the death penalty or a lifetime in jail, last night didn't go particularly well.

We needed information from Bradley, and I was hoping Marcus could get it. Now that is not going to happen; I doubt Bradley will say a word to the police, and from our point of view they would not even know what questions to ask.

In fact, I'm sure Bradley will not even be in New Jersey for long. Both Chicago and Vegas will want him extradited to their jurisdictions; I imagine Vegas will prevail because Bradley killed a cop there. But New Jersey will clearly not fight the extradition; this is not Somalia or Iran they are sending him to.

I've asked Laurie and Corey to use their contacts to learn the results of what would have been a search of Bradley's house; I particularly want to know if they've found his phone or the explosive device.

But I don't want to wait, particularly on the phone. I ask Eddie Dowd to request a subpoena for Bradley's phone call and phone GPS records, since we already know his number. We also know what the records will show, courtesy of Sam, but I need to get them legally so I can use them in court.

The cold truth is that we are still totally in the dark about the main questions that need to be answered. We don't know what Stanley Franklin's connection was to Bradley, Edwards, and whoever their bosses are. We don't know whether the explosion at Marstan last year was related to any of this, though Edwards did say that Bradley was involved in it. Most important, we don't know why Franklin was killed.

I've never fully bought into Jeff's belief that Franklin deliberately blew that building up. I'm not saying he wouldn't have killed those people; maybe they represented some kind of danger to him and he did it as an act of depraved self-preservation.

It's the artwork that was destroyed that makes his culpability unlikely in my eyes. By all accounts he loved fine works of art; it was his passion. It seems strange that he would destroy those paintings that were in the building. They didn't have to be there; he could have come up with some kind of reason to move them out well before the explosion, but he didn't.

I still wonder if it is possible that Franklin removed the paintings before the explosion and that the damage was so devastating that it was impossible to prove otherwise. The fire department captain said that the insurance company did not share my suspicions and wound up coughing up a lot of money.

Actually, I'm glad that Dietz brought up the explosion as a motive for Jeff. It opened the door for me to delve into it. Among other things, I can show that Jeff was a hero that day, and that he even saved a puppy! How bad could he be? There must be a bunch of puppy lovers on the jury.

But the source and purpose of the explosion is just one of the things I can't explain, and it is hard to present a coherent theory to the jury when I don't have any idea what I'm talking about.

The trial has not gone badly so far. Dietz's witnesses have mostly been for the purpose of setup, with only some referencing Jeff's grudge against Franklin. The exception to that was Jerry Cawley, and I am confident we successfully disposed of him.

Ultimately Cawley should prove to be helpful to us because clearly someone put him up to lying. Whoever did it must have offered him something; otherwise he would have had no incentive to testify. That means that someone outside the process wants Jeff convicted; if handled right, that alone should create suspicion in the minds of the jurors.

Hovering over everything is Bradley's acquisition of a detonator for an explosive device. It resulted in his having to deal with Marcus, which did not go well for him. Corey reported this morning that Bradley was taken to a hospital with a head injury, though he is expected to recover.

It also resulted in his capture. Had he not stiffed Charlie Silver out of $25,000, Silver would never have come forward with his whereabouts. I would like to have Silver testify, but there's no chance he would ever let that happen. I would also like to know why the hell Tony Bradley needed a detonator.

I'm going to try something this morning that will almost definitely not work, but if I don't, I would be violating the unwritten rule that states defense attorneys shall never miss an opportunity to throw shit against the wall and see if it sticks.

At my request, Eddie has filed a defense motion to suppress the evidence found in the dumpster belonging to Jeff's neighbor. It included the murder weapon and is the main piece of evidence tying Jeff to the crime.

Because the dumpster is privately owned, the police technically needed a warrant to search it. And because they never got one, we are contending that whatever they found should be suppressed.

It's a long-held legal doctrine called fruits of the poisonous tree, which means that evidence obtained as a result of illegal conduct cannot be admissible. In this case, searching without a warrant was the illegal conduct.

Judge Eddings decides to hear arguments on the motion before bringing the jury in this morning. I present our case, which is basically a verbalization of the motion.

"Your Honor, I understand that suppression of this material feels like a decision of huge consequence, but at its core the answer is obvious. This is why search warrants exist; to make an exception is what carries the greatest consequence. Police cannot search private property without a warrant, whether it is a safe, or a closet, or a dumpster. Private is private."

Dietz responds, "Your Honor, this is a frivolous motion. Assuming there was an error that was made here, it was a harmless one. The owner of the dumpster, Lawrence Brice, is not a suspect in this case. And because it is Mr. Brice's property, Mr. Wheeler cannot claim an expectation of privacy."

"So you are saying that a search warrant is of no consequence?" Eddings asks Dietz, with more skepticism than I anticipated.

Dietz shakes his head. "No, Your Honor. In most cases it is of paramount importance. But this is not one of those cases. There is no victim here."

"I can think of one, Your Honor," I say. "My client."

"Has Mr. Brice been informed that his rights were abrogated?" the judge asks.

"He is being contacted by a member of our staff right now," Dietz says.

"I want him more than contacted. If he is going to consent, albeit after the fact, I want to know about it. In the meantime, we can continue hearing testimony."

I still think we're going to lose one way or the other, but I'm surprised that Judge Eddings is taking this as seriously as she is.

I guess if you throw enough against the wall . . .

Once the jury is called in, Dietz's first witness is Captain Lee Hornstein of the Paramus Fire Department.

Captain Hornstein directed the response to the explosion at Marstan and the investigation afterward.

I've already interviewed him and pretty much know what he will say, and he sticks to the script. He says that the explosion was from a gas leak, and that there was no evidence at all that it was done deliberately.

Hornstein hasn't done us any damage; I'm not sure why Dietz called him. I suppose it's to show that Jeff was wrong in his accusations against Franklin, which might indicate that Jeff was not thinking clearly or was obsessed.

So to some degree I want to refute that. "Captain Hornstein, your written report on this matter said that the gas leak was of 'indeterminate origin.' Is that right?"

"Yes."

"Which means you know it was a gas leak, but you don't know what caused the leak?"

"Correct."

"You also said there was no evidence that it was a criminal act. Could it have been? Could someone have deliberately caused the leak and then set off a spark in some fashion which caused the explosion?"

"It's possible."

"So is it fair to say that not only is there no evidence that it was criminal, there is also no evidence that it was accidental?"

He nods. "That's fair."

"You said you've been on the job for nineteen years?"

"That's how long I've been with the department."

"And in that time, how many events similar to this gas leak explosion have you seen?"

"Two."

"You've been involved with investigating each one?"

"Yes . . . in various capacities."

"Did you determine that any of them were criminal?"

"No."

"Could they have been, but the evidence was destroyed in the blasts?"

"Certainly possible. The damage in each case was very extensive."

"How does the amount of damage factor in?" I ask.

"Well, imagine you have a pipe with a leak in it. Then further imagine that you surround that pipe with dynamite and destroy it . . . you blow it to bits. Then you engulf it in fire. Would you be able to determine exactly where the leak was and what caused it?"

I smile. "I don't think I could. Is this what happened at Marstan?"

"Yes."

"So that's why you said it was of 'indeterminate origin'?"

"Yes. Massive explosions tend to make analysis difficult."

"Thank you."

Next up for the prosecution is Sergeant Susan Casper, who works in the cybercrime unit of the police department. Jeff's computer had been confiscated after his arrest.

"You have had an opportunity to thoroughly analyze the defendant's computer?" Dietz asks.

"We have."

"Please tell us what you found, limiting it to matters relevant to this case and concerning Stanley Franklin."

Casper spends the next fifteen minutes detailing what she uncovered. Most of it consists of emails that Jeff sent to various authorities demanding that the question of Franklin's culpability in the explosion be investigated.

He was consistently rebuffed, and his responses became more and more strident. One can feel his frustration building as he gets nowhere. In total he comes across as someone truly obsessed, which I fear in the jurors' minds will indicate someone capable of murder.

"And this represents only a small portion of the emails he sent on the subject?" Dietz asks.

Casper nods. "Definitely less than half."

Most damaging is her analysis of Jeff's Google searches. A lot of them over the past year were seeking information on gas leak explosions, but one a week before the murder is particularly troubling.

"There was a search for Mr. Franklin's home address. It was on one of those sites that provide private information in return for payment."

"So he paid for the victim's home address?"

"Yes. He used his credit card."

That's clearly the information that Dietz was after, and he turns the witness over to me. I've already discussed this with Jeff, so I am prepared for how to cross-examine Casper. "Sergeant, among the emails you did not show, were there any that spoke about potential legal actions the defendant might take against Mr. Franklin?"

"Yes. A number of them. He told a few people he was going to sue, mainly so he would be able to put Franklin under oath. Also, in the three weeks before the murder he attempted to recruit two lawyers to his cause."

"So he was actively considering a lawsuit at that point?"

"Yes."

"Did he ever mention the possibility of murdering Mr. Franklin instead?"

"No. Not in these emails."

"When one files a lawsuit, if you know, how does one inform the defendant in the action that he is being sued?"

"I believe a subpoena is served."

"If you were planning to serve a subpoena on someone at their house, would it be helpful to know their address?"

"I suppose so."

"You suppose so?"

"Yes."

"Then I suppose I don't have any further questions."

The afternoon session starts off on a down note, though a predictable one.

While we were in session, Dietz's people have gotten a retroactive consent from the homeowner who owned the dumpster in which the gun was found.

That essentially eliminated the need for a warrant, and Judge Eddings has no choice but to overrule my motion for suppression. She must be relieved; to dismiss this case would have exposed her to intense criticism and in the public's minds would potentially have put a murderer back on the street.

I'm not terribly disappointed since I expected this result. We fought the good fight and lost.

Dietz's next witness is Amanda Rieger. She is a waitress at Ricardo's Steak House in Fort Lee. Dietz quickly establishes that she was there the night that Jeff threatened Franklin.

"Who was Mr. Franklin dining with?"

"His wife and Wilson Paul."

"Who is Wilson Paul, if you know?"

"I believe he works at Mr. Franklin's company. I was told that, but I'm not sure."

"You'd waited on them before?"

"Oh, yes. Mr. Franklin was a regular, and his wife and Mr. Paul were often with him. Not always all three together, though."

"I understand. At any point did Mr. Wheeler walk over to their table?"

"Yes, I was serving their entrées at the time. I looked over and he was there . . . everybody at the table seemed surprised."

"Had Mr. Wheeler been dining there?"

"No. He came in, saw Mr. Franklin at the table, and came right over. I don't believe he had a reservation or was planning to eat."

"What happened next?" Dietz asks.

"Mr. Wheeler started screaming at him. He said Mr. Franklin was a murderer and that he would be exposed. He said that his time was coming, that he could not get away with what he did."

"Did Mr. Franklin or anyone else at the table say anything?"

"No, at least not that I heard. The restaurant manager and a couple of the waiters came over and took Mr. Wheeler outside."

There isn't much for me to get on cross-examination. "Ms. Rieger, you testified that Mr. Wheeler said that the truth about Mr. Franklin would be exposed?"

"Yes."

"He didn't mention that physical violence would come to him?"

"No, but he was really angry."

"Please just answer my questions."

"Sorry."

"Did Mr. Wheeler attack Mr. Franklin? Did he lunge at him? Punch him?"

"No."

"Did he have to be physically restrained from attacking him?"

"No."

"When the manager and waiters came over, did Mr. Wheeler resist?"

"No."

"He left peacefully?"

"Yes."

"He didn't have to be dragged out?"

"No."

"And he never put a hand on Mr. Franklin the whole time?"

"He did not."

"Thank you. No further questions."

Rieger's testimony has been damaging... no doubt about it. Jeff came off as furious, if not deranged, for having accosted Franklin so publicly.

Dietz calls two more witnesses, both essentially fillers, to use up time. They both testify that Jeff had discussed with them his feelings about Franklin and his belief that Franklin caused the explosion deliberately.

They don't cause us any great or additional harm; they're just more of the same. Dietz obviously wants to save his big gun for tomorrow morning, and these witnesses were designed to bridge the gap.

When I get home, Laurie gives me an interesting, though not surprising, piece of news. The police found a handgun in Bradley's house and ran ballistics tests on it. It was a positive match for the gun used to kill Nick Edwards.

That's going to help us, and we're going to need it.

If I'm right, Dietz will put on one more witness, which means we need to be ready to start the defense case tomorrow.

His witness will deliver what he hopes will be the clincher, the forensic evidence relating to the plastic bag in the dumpster. We'll poke at it, but won't get far.

I'm basically pleased with our case; I think we have a decent chance to raise reasonable-doubt issues. My problem is more about my lack of understanding of what is behind all of this.

The questions I had at the beginning of our investigation remain largely unanswered, with just two exceptions. Those exceptions are important. We now know who actually killed Franklin. It was Tony Bradley; we have his phone a couple of blocks from the murder scene, and we have Nick Edwards telling us that Bradley left the car and walked to the house.

We also know, or at least we're pretty sure, that Jeff was right and the explosion at Marstan Industries was set off deliberately. He was certain that Franklin was behind it, but all we know for sure is the comment from Edwards that Bradley was involved. Maybe Bradley did it at Franklin's direction, or just his concurrence; that is unclear. But it was not an accident.

We don't know why they blew up the building, why Franklin was killed, or why Bradley and his bosses bought that new detonator. Technically we don't have to know any of that to effectively present our case, but I wish we did.

I am always more comfortable presenting facts when I know the reasons behind them. It just helps me argue more effectively. And it makes our story more believable.

I get home and take the dogs on a long walk through the park. I don't know if Marcus is watching out for me, or if there is any need for him to do so. Edwards is dead and Bradley is in custody. Hopefully that eliminates all the threats, but then again violent thugs seem to be a renewable resource. And Edwards did say that Bradley had a dangerous partner.

"Big day tomorrow," I say to Tara, Hunter, and Rufus. They don't respond, but I can tell by their solemn attitude that they understand the importance of the situation.

"Especially for you, Rufus. We want to get your dad home. But should it not go well, you don't have to worry. You'll always be safe with us."

I think Rufus appreciates that, but he doesn't get a chance to show it because he sees a squirrel. Once the squirrel is safely up a tree, I let the leashes go so the three of them can bark at the squirrel in vain as it taunts them from above.

After a few minutes they give up and we move on.

Life can be simple when your only goal is to catch a squirrel.

Lieutenant Carl Richardson takes the stand. He's functioned as the lead detective on the case.

I don't know much about him other than that Pete Stanton told me at Charlie's he is a terrific cop whose mere presence will insure my humiliating defeat.

I am lucky to have such supportive friends.

"I've been a police officer for twenty-four years, the last sixteen in the Homicide Division," Richardson says.

Dietz has him list all the commendations he has gotten; if it embarrasses Richardson, he's hiding it well.

"And you were the lead detective on the investigation into the murder of Stanley Franklin?"

"Yes, sir."

"You were on the scene that night?"

"Yes, I arrived approximately thirty-one minutes after the initial nine-one-one call. We were alerted that there was a homicide by the officers on the scene."

Dietz has him describe what he saw when he arrived, which is no different from what everyone else saw, and what the photos show.

Richardson describes how he had the premises thoroughly searched and sent officers out to canvass the area and see if neighbors reported seeing anything unusual. Then he interviewed Margaret Franklin.

"She was still quite upset, as would be expected," Richardson says. "It took a while before she could compose herself enough to talk to me."

"What did she say?"

"That the doorbell rang, which was unusual at night, since they were not expecting anyone. Mr. and Mrs. Franklin were in an upstairs bedroom, and Mr. Franklin went down to answer the door.

"She reported hearing the door open and Mr. Franklin say, 'What the hell are you doing here?' or words to that effect. She did not hear a response and in fact heard nothing else for what she said was three or four minutes.

"She then went downstairs, found Mr. Franklin lying there, and called nine one one."

"So she did not hear any gunshots?"

"She said she did not."

"What else did you ask her?"

"If she had any idea who could have done this. At first she said she did not. But then I asked her if Mr. Franklin had any enemies, and she remembered an incident from the night before.

"She said Jeffrey Wheeler had loudly threatened Mr. Franklin in a restaurant the previous night, and that he had been harassing Mr. Franklin for months with unfounded accusations."

"Is that how you came to view Mr. Wheeler as a suspect?"

"Yes."

"What did you do?"

"We went to his house and brought him in for questioning, but he refused to talk with us. We executed a search warrant on his house and searched the surrounding area as well."

"Did you find anything relevant?"

"Yes. In a dumpster owned by a neighbor on the next block."

Dietz painstakingly takes Richardson through his description of what was in the bag . . . all the personal items related to Jeff and, most important, the gun.

Jeff's DNA was all over it, and they even did a handwriting analysis on the grocery list.

It takes almost an hour to go through everything, but it feels like a month. Dietz wraps it up with "Did you run a ballistics test on the gun?"

"We did. It was a positive match for the weapon that was used to kill Stanley Franklin."

Ouch.

My turn. "Lieutenant, you said that Mrs. Franklin recounted the confrontation between Mr. Wheeler and Mr. Franklin in the restaurant, is that correct?"

"Yes. She also talked of the ongoing harassment by Wheeler."

"Had you ever heard of Mr. Wheeler before that conversation with Mrs. Franklin? Were you familiar with him in any way?"

"No."

"But just based on what she said, you were focused enough on Mr. Wheeler to secure and execute a search warrant on his house?"

"Yes."

"So the length of time that you investigated before settling on a suspect was how long, about three or four seconds?"

"The length of time is not important; the facts are what matter."

"Fine, but I would appreciate it if you could answer my question without lecturing the court on what is important. How long did it take for your investigation to yield this suspect? Mrs. Franklin said what she said, and you went, 'Hey, wait a second, we have a suspect.' Is that how it happened? So just a few seconds?"

Dietz objects that I'm badgering the witness, which of course I am, so when Judge Eddings sustains, I move on.

"How far is it from Mr. Franklin's house to Mr. Wheeler's house?"

"I didn't measure it."

"Ballpark it . . . maybe ten miles?"

"Sounds about right."

"So is it your theory of the case that Mr. Wheeler shot Mr. Franklin and then drove twenty miles to throw away the gun one block from his house?"

"That's what happened."

"No, that's your theory as to what happened. Or were you in the car when he did it?"

"I was not."

"So Mr. Wheeler drove all that distance only to dispose of the gun near his house. Then is it also your theory that he said to himself, 'Wait a minute. I need to make it clearer that I did this, so I'm going to include a whole bunch of stuff that's mine, including my grocery list.' Is that how you see it?"

"That is what happened."

I frown as if frustrated and shake my head. "No, that's your theory as to what happened. Do you always have trouble distinguishing between theory and fact?"

Dietz objects and the judge sustains with a warning to me. Ho hum.

"Now, moving right along, you said some of the items had Mr. Wheeler's fingerprints on them, mainly because they were his, and he put them in the bag using his fingers. But you didn't mention anything about fingerprints on the gun. Were his prints on the gun?"

"There were no prints on the gun. It was wiped clean."

"So everything else in the bag was put in by Mr. Wheeler using his fingers and hands, but he beamed the gun in there?"

"He might have used gloves," Richardson says.

"Did you find the gloves?"

"No."

"Is it your theory that he had all these things in the bag that could clearly identify him, but he was worried about fingerprints on the gun?"

"I can't speak to any mistakes that he made."

"Can you speak to all the mistakes that you made?"

"That's your characterization. We got the right man."

"Lieutenant, are you aware that phones can be located by a GPS contained within them?"

"Of course."

"That's a tool now commonly used in law enforcement, correct?"

"Yes."

"Did you check to see if Mr. Wheeler's phone was near Mr. Franklin's house that night?"

"Yes. It was not."

"So if he was there, he didn't bring his phone?"

"It could have been shut off."

"Did you look at other phones in the area around that time?"

"Yes, within a one-block radius."

"And found nothing suspicious?"

"Correct."

"So you figure he was smart enough to prevent you from tracking his phone, but dumb enough to put the murder weapon next to his grocery list?"

"Criminals make mistakes. That's why the prisons are filled with them."

"Do police detectives ever make mistakes?"

"Of course."

"Lieutenant Richardson, just between you and I, and the jury, and Judge Eddings, don't you wish you had conducted a competent investigation?"

Dietz objects, Judge Eddings admonishes me, and I withdraw the question and excuse the witness. It feels like all this has happened before.

Once Richardson is off the stand, Dietz rises. "Your Honor, the prosecution rests."

This was the first time Margaret Franklin had been to the Marstan offices since her husband's murder.

She was there to meet at the request of Wilson Paul, and she wasn't looking forward to it. Business matters bored her; she had always resisted Stanley's half-hearted efforts to get her more involved.

Paul hadn't said what the meeting was about, but she assumed it was either company issues, or more likely a large off-site meeting they had planned for the near future. Paul had previously asked her to be there and say a few words, to demonstrate continuity. She had turned him down and assumed he now wanted to press the issue.

"Nice to see you, Margaret," Paul said when she was brought back to his office. "I appreciate your coming down."

"I see you've taken Stanley's office."

He smiled. "No sense letting it go to waste. He won't be back anytime soon."

His comment surprised her. "That was crude."

"Sorry. It slipped out," he said in a tone that indicated he wasn't sorry at all.

Margaret Franklin was quickly becoming annoyed with

his attitude, and more than a little puzzled. This seemed uncharacteristic for Paul; he usually vacillated between ingratiating and obsequious. But now that Stanley was no longer around, maybe things had changed.

Well, she would change them back. "What is it you want, Wilson?"

"A larger piece of the proceeds from the art auction."

"Excuse me?"

"Which part didn't you hear? I want a larger piece of the proceeds from the art auction. Significantly larger."

"Based on what?"

"Well, let's see, to start we can say it's based on the fact that I know what Stanley was doing, and exactly how you are going to make a fortune."

"That's insane."

"Whatever; let's get this over with. Just pick up the phone and call that wimpy guy at the auction house." Paul picked up a piece of paper from his desk and handed it to her. "I've written down the new terms so you won't have to remember them."

"I see that," she said, looking at them. "Wilson, I don't know what you are talking about, and if this stops now, I will try and pretend we never had this conversation. Otherwise I will terminate your employment effective immediately."

"I don't think you understand, Margaret. I said I know everything. And all I have to do is go to the media, or even better, the police, and you are finished."

"You're crazy."

He proceeded to tell her what he knew, to demonstrate

that he was not crazy. "I have all the leverage here, Margaret."

"So you do," she says, stunned at the turn of events.

He pointed to the phone. "Make the call."

I'm going to start our defense by focusing on the explosion.

It's the least important part of the case, in that it has no direct bearing on the Franklin murder. No matter what the truth is about that night, it does not mean that Jeff could not have killed Franklin.

But the prosecution dwelled on it as a motive and attempted, with no evidence to justify it, to make Jeff sound obsessed to the point of being out of control with rage. I need to go at that.

I call Kirsten Lillis, whose husband, Gary, was one of the Marstan employees killed in the explosion. Once I've established this, I ask what Gary's role was.

"He was vice president of finance. He spent four years there."

"Mr. Wheeler's girlfriend, Lisa Dozier, was one of the people who worked in his department?"

Lillis nods. "Yes. She reported to Gary."

"Did you have occasion to meet Mr. Wheeler?"

"Yes. After the . . . incident . . . he joined the other families in our efforts to decide what to do. But since he was not a family member, some people felt his role was different. For example, he wouldn't be legally able to share in any financial settlement."

"Did you know he blamed Stanley Franklin for the explosion? That he thought it was done intentionally?"

"Yes."

"Did you agree with that?"

"I wasn't sure; I'm still not. But I am very suspicious."

"Why is that?"

"Gary had been upset about something work related, to a level I had never seen before. He wouldn't say exactly what it was, just that they had discovered something about Franklin and they were going to confront him that night."

"Was Gary worried about his reaction?"

"Oh, yes. He thought it could cost them their jobs."

"Is there any other reason for your suspicion?"

"Yes. Franklin was supposed to be there that night for this meeting; it was the only reason the meeting was being held. But he never showed up, and afterwards he lied about it. He said he didn't even know about the meeting. I mean, why would he lie unless he had something to hide?"

"Did Gary tell you verbally that Franklin was going to come to the meeting, and that they were going to confront him about whatever it was they had learned?"

"Yes, but he also wrote me an email that day. . . ."

I introduce the email into evidence, which basically supports everything she said, and then ask, "In your dealings with Mr. Wheeler, did he ever refer to the possibility of physical violence against Mr. Franklin?"

"No."

"Thank you," I say, before turning her over to Dietz.

He clearly wants to treat her delicately, in deference to her status as a grieving widow. "Mrs. Lillis, I am sorry for your terrible loss."

"Thank you."

"I understand you have suspicions about Mr. Franklin regarding that night, but do you have any actual evidence that shows he may have deliberately destroyed his own building?"

"Only what I've said so far."

Dietz nods. "But other than the suspicions that you say you shared with Mr. Wheeler, did he ever show you any actual evidence?"

"No."

"Thank you."

Next I call Jenna Landry, the friend of another victim and Rufus's former owner, Cynthia Wilmore. She talks about how Cynthia always brought Rufus to work, and she would never have put him in a cage in the lobby, as she did that night, if it wasn't that her boss was going to be in their meeting.

Dietz pretty much dismisses her, coming up with a number of behavioral reasons why Rufus could have been relegated to the cage. He has obviously never met Rufus.

He also shows that Landry has no concrete evidence whatsoever that Franklin was supposed to be there that night, and obviously none that he intentionally blew up the building.

My final witness for the day is Kyle Bourne, a worker

in a building not far from Marstan, who ran to the scene when he heard the explosion. He describes how he saw Jeff run into the burning building, come out with the little puppy, and try to run back in.

He describes it in heroic terms, which are justified. Dietz, of course, is not interested in dwelling on Jeff's heroism. He simply gets Bourne to admit that what Jeff did that day has nothing to do with whether he killed someone a year later.

It has not been an auspicious start for our side, but there were boxes we needed to check.

Tomorrow is our big day . . . hopefully.

"Wallace, I have some changes to make in the distribution of funds once the auction is complete," Margaret Franklin said.

She was calling Linder at Echelon to dictate the changes. What Linder did not know, of course, was that she was doing it under a blackmail threat from Wilson Paul. Linder also had no way of knowing that she was calling from Paul's office as he listened to what she had to say.

"Oh?" Linder asked.

"Yes, I'll be sending you a letter memorializing it, but I wanted you to know."

"Obviously you can allocate your share however you like, Margaret."

"Thank you."

"Interest from bidders has been very significant and is growing."

"Glad to hear it."

"It will be an exciting day. Historic, really."

"Good. Thank you, Wallace. Good-bye."

She hung up before waiting for him to say good-bye. He saw that as strange. He saw everything about the call as strange. But with Franklin's death, she was the boss, so he'd do what she wanted.

At the end of the day, Linder didn't care how she allocated her share.

It was his share that he cared about.

I need to make Tony Bradley famous today.

There is no way I can convince the jury that Jeff did not kill Stanley Franklin without making them believe that someone else might have. That someone else is Tony Bradley.

The truth is that I'm not creating a fantasy; Bradley really was the shooter. I know that because Nick Edwards sat with him in the car that night and watched him walk to the Franklin house. He wasn't going there to wish Franklin a pleasant evening.

I also know, courtesy of Nick Edwards, that Bradley was involved in setting off the explosion at Marstan that killed the seven people. I further know, courtesy of Charlie Silver, that Bradley spent $25,000 to purchase a detonator, though I don't know why.

Of course, the detonator might have nothing to do with our case. This might not be the only illegal activity that Bradley was involved in. He could have been simultaneously working for someone else on a completely different matter. Maybe Bradley was a criminal multitasker.

The problem is that I can't get any of this before the jury. Anything Edwards told us is hearsay and therefore not admissible, and we have no proof that he said it. There are exceptional circumstances in which hearsay testimony is acceptable, but this situation does not meet any of those conditions.

And Charlie Silver will never let himself be found and wouldn't testify anyway. He would be incriminating himself by admitting he had built and supplied the detonator. Charlie is not the self-incriminating type.

So I'm stuck between what I know for a fact and what I can tell the jury. It is extremely frustrating.

When Jeff is brought into court, he looks more nervous than usual. "Big day today, right?"

I nod. "Big day."

Eddie puts his hand on Jeff's shoulder; Eddie's been instrumental in keeping Jeff calm and on an even keel all along. "Sit back and enjoy the fun," Eddie says. "But don't smile or nod while you're doing it."

My first witness is Sergeant Dave Kramer, who works for Pete Stanton in the Homicide Division of the Paterson PD. I know and like Kramer, and while that "like" is probably unrequited, I do believe that he's one of the few cops in the department that doesn't despise me.

I direct him to the morning that Edwards's body was found in Pennington Park. "Sergeant Kramer, how did you come to be in the park that morning?"

"A nine-one-one call was made indicating that a couple walking in the park found a dead body. Officers went to the scene, determined it was a homicide, and my partner and I were dispatched to begin the investigation."

"What did you find when you arrived?"

"A Caucasian male, later to be identified as Nicholas Edwards, was deceased and had obviously been shot in the head. The coroner later confirmed the bullet wound as the cause of death."

"In your investigation, what did you learn about Nick Edwards?"

"I guess you could describe him as a career criminal. Frequent arrests, two jail terms, always either in trouble or looking to find a way to get into trouble. Not a model citizen."

"At any point did you confiscate Mr. Edwards's phone?"

"No, it was neither on his body nor at his home."

I'm not surprised by that since Marcus took both of his phones and gave them to Sam, but I don't think I'll mention that. "Did you examine the records of his registered cell phone, both for his calls and for the GPS locations?"

"We did."

"What did you learn, limiting yourself to facts relevant to this trial, please."

"Mr. Edwards was at a location in Alpine, New Jersey, approximately two and a half blocks from Stanley Franklin's house."

"When was that?"

"Just around the time of the murder of Mr. Franklin."

"How long was his phone there?"

"Almost an hour."

I put up on the screen two pages of Edwards's phone records and ask Kramer to note a particular number. "Who does that phone belong to?"

"It's registered to a Ms. Dierdre Millman."

"Sergeant, did I also ask you to review the cell phone records for Stanley Franklin in the two weeks before his death?"

Kramer nods. "Yes, and I did so."

"Had Mr. Franklin ever called Ms. Millman?"

"Yes, a number of times."

"Did you investigate who Dierdre Millman is? Where she lives? Where she works?"

"We did. We came up empty in all cases. There is no Dierdre Millman."

"I don't understand," I say, even though I obviously do. "I thought you said she owns that phone."

"It is a fake name with a fake address. There is no such person."

"So just to sum up, both Nick Edwards and Stanley Franklin were in touch with the same person, on a phone belonging to someone who does not exist?"

"That's correct."

Dietz stands to question Kramer; if Dietz isn't worried, he should be.

"Sergeant, you said you couldn't find Mr. Edwards's phone, correct?"

"Yes."

"Not on his person, or in his house, or in his car?"

"That's right. It is still missing."

"Now all these calls, and all these locations that you talked about, you don't know if Mr. Edwards made those calls or was in those locations, do you?"

"No, I can only speak to the phone itself."

"Anyone could have had and used the phone?"

"Yes, it's possible. I don't know if it had a code to open it or not," Kramer says.

"So you don't know if Edwards himself was in Alpine, or if he called this Dierdre Millman person, whoever she is?"

"That's right."

"Have you done any investigative work on this case? The one this jury is here to decide?"

"I have not."

"Thank you, Sergeant."

There was fairly intense media interest, and therefore public interest, in the Jeff Wheeler trial.

Ironically, the person who might have been thought to be the one following it most closely did not care how it ended.

It didn't matter to Margaret Franklin whether Jeff Wheeler was found guilty or not guilty. It would not change her life one way or the other, and her life was fine the way it was.

She knew that the purpose of framing Wheeler had been to avoid further investigation into finding the killer and the motive behind it. That no longer mattered.

If Wheeler was exonerated and the police took up the investigation again, they would quickly settle on Tony Bradley as the perpetrator. The lawyer, Carpenter, would lead them in that direction.

Margaret had no confidence in people at all; no expectations that they would be smart or honorable. So she was rarely surprised by anything that anyone did.

Wilson Paul was the exception to that. Not that he had turned on her and blackmailed her; she knew he was perfectly capable of that, if big money was at stake. She had not expected him to be smart enough to figure some things out.

Of course, he had no idea just how much money was at stake. On a previous phone call—not the one that Wilson Paul listened in on—Wallace Linder had told her the bid that was going to come in and who the bidder was going to be. It was a staggering amount that would blow all the other potential buyers out of the water.

So while Paul had proven to be more intelligent and savvy than Margaret had thought, she was aware of his key mistake. He thought he knew everything, when in fact he did not. And that would prove to be his undoing.

And as for the success of the conspiracy that the frame-up of Wheeler was meant to insure, nothing could derail it anymore.

It was so close she could touch it.

I am still trying to understand the motivation for blowing up the Marstan building, and I'm starting to feel desperate about it.

I know with some certainty that there is a connection between that event and the Franklin murder; Tony Bradley was involved in both. So I have felt all along that if I could find the motivation for one, I'd find it for the other.

In my mind there are three possibilities, three things that Bradley and whoever he was working for could have wanted to accomplish in destroying that building.

One is to destroy the artwork that Franklin kept there. It was extremely valuable, and the insurance payoff on the paintings could have solved a bunch of problems for Franklin, whose business had been experiencing difficulties. He also had a big loan to pay back, though I don't know the source of that loan, or why there is no evidence it has been repaid, in full or part.

I've tried to look at the destroyed artwork from every angle. What if the paintings were stolen? That seems impossible because no victims have come forward. These are extraordinarily valuable pieces, and in some cases well-known. Would someone not have claimed them if they had been stolen?

And what if they were forged, if that's even possible? I have to assume that great care had been taken to confirm that they were legitimate. For instance, when it comes to the paintings up for auction at Echelon, two sets of experts and the Metropolitan Museum vouched for their authenticity.

They even used something called radioactive carbon dating. I don't know what that is, and my experience with dating in the past was not all that successful, but I'll take their word for it.

Lastly, what if the artwork was not there at all? Could it secretly have been removed before the explosion? Would enough material have survived to have been identifiable in the ashes afterward? I make a note to again ask the fire department captain about that possibility. Maybe this time I'll get a different answer.

But if it wasn't the art, then the target could have been the people that were gathered for that meeting. They had discovered something troubling and were so concerned that the plan was to confront Franklin, who was their boss, that night.

Lisa Dozier had said to Jeff that what they had discovered could be criminal, and I also have testimony that the group felt it was significant enough that they could lose their jobs for revealing it. Maybe whatever it was represented such a major threat to Franklin that it was decided the seven people had to be eliminated.

The last possibility, and I think the least likely one, is

that the target was Franklin himself. By all accounts he was supposed to be at that meeting; perhaps Bradley and his bosses were getting rid of him. It didn't work because Franklin didn't show up for the meeting, but they finished the job with the shooting at his house, albeit a year later.

The logic fails, though, in that there would have been far easier ways to stage an "accident" causing Franklin's death. He could have died in a hit-and-run or any of countless other ways; destroying the building and killing seven people is obviously extreme and literally overkill.

Much of my problem in figuring out what is going on is that I don't know how Franklin was involved. Was he calling the shots? Was he taking orders from others? Was he an equal partner, but he began causing problems and he was eliminated?

Knowing whether Franklin directed or approved the destruction of the building is key to knowing the motivation behind it. I find it hard to imagine that he was fine with the destruction of the precious paintings that were his obsession, which would mean that the decision to do it was someone else's.

But if Franklin was involved in something illegal and desperately feared exposure by the seven people, then he could at least have gone along with it. And there was always the insurance money to ease the pain.

All of this has been a puzzle I've been trying to solve ever since I got involved in this case. But the pressure to solve it has increased and intensified as the trial is coming to an end.

Because once the case goes to the jury, it's too late.

In my entire career I don't think I've ever called two police officers in a row to testify for the defense.

But desperate times call for desperate measures.

I'm sure the officers aren't thrilled about it either; they could get drummed out of the Society for the Hatred of Defense Attorneys. But they are here; I'd like to think it is out of the goodness of their hearts, but just in case, I sent them subpoenas.

I call Jake Fletcher of the Ridgewood Police Department. He is the detective who handled the Tony Bradley arrest, though not too much detecting was necessary. Marcus knocked out Bradley in his house and a neighbor's phone call brought the cops to the scene where they picked him up.

"Detective, did you arrest a man named Tony Bradley last week?"

"Yes."

"How did you come to do that?"

"A former Paterson police officer named Corey Douglas knew of his location and contacted one of our officers. Mr. Bradley was in his home, and officers went to the scene and placed him into custody."

That's the sanitized version that the arriving cop who knew Corey must have peddled. It's fine with me.

"Was Mr. Bradley injured in the course of making the arrest?"

"He was, but his injuries were not serious. He recovered quickly."

"What did he do that prompted his arrest?"

"He had warrants out for him in Chicago and Las Vegas. They were both for murder, and the victim in Las Vegas was a police officer. He had been on the run for more than a year."

"Where is he today?"

"He was extradited to Nevada, where he will face murder charges."

"Was a search conducted of his home after he was taken into custody?"

"Yes."

"Was his phone recovered in that search?"

"Yes."

"Was it registered in his name? Tony Bradley?"

"No, it was registered in the name of Dierdre Millman. We found no such person; the name and listed address were fake."

"I see. As you know, the defense subpoenaed the records from his phone. I've asked you to familiarize yourself with what those records show. Have you done that?"

"Yes, I have."

"Please summarize what you learned, limiting it to things that relate to this case."

"At one point the phone was in Alpine, New Jersey,

within two blocks of the house owned by Stanley and Margaret Franklin."

"That's the Stanley Franklin who is the victim in the case we are trying?" I ask, just in case the jurors are not real bright.

"Yes."

"When was the phone there?"

"Right around the time of Mr. Franklin's murder. It was there for approximately one hour."

"Detective, there has been previous testimony that the phone belonging to Nick Edwards was in the same location at the same time. Is there any way to know if the two people possessing these phones were together?"

"No way to tell that, but they clearly were not far apart."

"Do you know the purpose of their being there? Maybe they were attending a slimeball convention?"

"I can't speak to their reason for being there."

"As a detective, do you find it suspicious?"

"I do."

"Detective, did Mr. Bradley ever make a call to or receive calls from Mr. Edwards's phone?"

"Yes, on a number of occasions."

"Did Mr. Franklin ever make calls to or receive calls from Mr. Bradley's phone?"

"Yes, also on a number of occasions."

"So, just to be clear. Stanley Franklin was in contact with two men, one of whom is a career criminal, and the other of whom was a wanted killer? A wanted cop killer?"

"That is correct."

"Do you have any idea what the reason was for this

three-way grouping? Maybe they were all in the same book club?"

"I do not."

"Thank you."

I thought that went well; my only concern is whether the jury was able to follow it. I am going to have to make it clear in my closing statement.

Dietz takes the same tack he did with Sergeant Kramer. He implies that this is much ado about nothing, and that the location of phones reveals nothing relevant to why we are here.

I'm sitting at the defense table and I'm worried. The testimony of the two officers went as well as I could have hoped. Among other things, they placed a murderer, Tony Bradley, very close to the scene of the crime.

What else could he have been doing in that exclusive Alpine neighborhood that night? Attending a Tupperware party? A PTA meeting? The implications of his presence should be obvious.

And the witnesses also proved a connection between Bradley and Edwards, as well as Bradley and Franklin. Franklin was involved with bad people, one of them a murderer. How could the jury be certain he did not die because of that involvement?

But my worry is not just my natural pessimism, though I'm sure that's a part of it. I'm afraid I've buried the jury with arcane facts about cell phone logs and GPS coordinates, and they're probably putting that to the side and saying, "Maybe, but the damn murder weapon was sitting in a bag with his grocery list."

I've discussed with Jeff the idea of his testifying in his own defense. Like all innocent people, his inclination is to take the stand and proclaim that innocence to the world. But he was willing to follow my advice, which was for him not to go anywhere near that witness stand.

There is not a single fact that he has evidence to refute. He doesn't know how the material wound up in that dumpster, he clearly did hold a grudge against Franklin, and he absolutely threatened him in the restaurant the night before the killing.

So what is he going to say? That he didn't do it? How would that help his cause? All it would accomplish would be to give Dietz an opportunity to take him apart on cross-examination. I can almost see him at the prosecution table salivating at the prospect.

So right now I'm wishing I could put Jeff on the stand, only because I don't want the defense case to end. I don't think I've done enough, and ending my case means I am giving up control.

But it would be stupid and counterproductive to put him up there, so I won't. Instead I stand and say the words that I always hate to hear come out of my mouth.

"Your Honor, the defense rests."

The detonator that Charlie Silver had produced for Tony Bradley had not been found.

The police had searched his premises and his car for any incriminating material, and neither the detonator nor the explosive device it was meant to attach to had turned up.

Of course, the cops had not specifically been looking for it; they weren't even sure it existed. Charlie Silver had revealed it to Andy Carpenter and his team and then disappeared.

Carpenter had told the police he heard from confidential sources that Bradley might have had a bomb, but the police did not take that particularly seriously. Carpenter showed them no real evidence to support it, and they assumed it could be a defense attorney posturing to improve his case.

But the reason it had not been found was that it was already in position, in what could be described as its final resting place. It was in a now-locked closet in the Echelon building, effectively concealed by boxes and used canvases.

It had been brought in soon after Bradley received it, aided by the lack of metal detectors and the generally inadequate security at the entrance to the building. No one in authority had noticed anything and now they never would.

The device would sit in that closet until spurred into action by a simple phone call.

No one would find it.

No one would know about it.

Until it was too late.

My closing argument in this case is going to be the most important I can ever remember.

Usually, my role is to sum up what the jury has heard in terms most favorable to our side. I have to remind the jurors about the mountains of exculpatory evidence that have been presented and educate them on what they missed while they were dozing off.

I also have to tell them exactly why the incriminating evidence that the prosecution has presented is basically worthless and should be rejected with extreme prejudice.

But this time is a bit different. I have to assume that the jury heard what we had to say, but may not have fully understood it. So I have to make crystal clear why the phone records and GPS logs prove Jeff's innocence or at least provide the necessary reasonable doubt about his guilt.

In other words, I have to tell them to forget all about the grudges and the threats and the fingerprints and the DNA and the murder weapon. No sense in their looking over there; instead they should focus on these phone-company records I have over here.

Tonight I am treating myself to a dinner out with Laurie

and Ricky. It's been a while since we've done this; murder cases tend to prevent real-life activities.

We go to a new seafood restaurant in Fort Lee that was recently included on some magazine's list as one of the best restaurants in the Northeast. How do they do that? Does one enormous person sample every restaurant in the Northeast?

It turns out to be very good, but I can't say it's worthy of that kind of recognition. Of course, as my mother used to eloquently put it, "Fish is fish."

But the desserts are terrific and so is the fact that we laugh throughout the meal. I don't think about the case except constantly, but I'm also able to have a good time with my favorite people in the world.

It's a rare treat, and when we get home, I cap it off with a long walk with Tara, Hunter, and Rufus. Laurie and Ricky come along, though they refuse to carry and use the plastic bag.

Apparently family loyalty extends only so far.

The gallery is packed but remarkably quiet as Dietz stands to give his closing argument.

Everyone recognizes that this is it, once we're done, it's going to be out of our hands and into the jury's twenty-four grubby paws. I'm going to be speaking to these people, cajoling and convincing, and then there is a good chance I am going to hate them afterward.

"Ladies and gentlemen, this has felt like a long journey, hasn't it?" Dietz asks, and a few of the jurors smile in response. "These sessions have been pressure packed, demanding your full concentration, and days like that feel longer than most.

"So I thank you for your attention, for putting up with we lawyers as we've rambled on and on, and for listening carefully to the witnesses and evidence.

"So I want to talk about that evidence. But first, if you'll forgive me, a little background. There are various elements in any criminal trial, things we as prosecutors like to convey to a jury. They are in different ways essential to proving guilt beyond a reasonable doubt.

"The first is motive. It's a little-known fact that prosecutors do not have to demonstrate motive; legally it's unnecessary. But I'll let you in on a secret . . . we always want to. We think it's tough to ask someone to identify a guilty party without revealing why they did it.

"In this case, the motive is clear; the defendant literally screamed it out at a restaurant. He tragically lost his girlfriend, likely his future wife, in a terrible accident. He blamed Stanley Franklin and accused him of deliberately blowing up his own building.

"Now, please understand this. While there is no evidence that Mr. Franklin did this, whether he did or not actually doesn't matter. What matters is that the defendant believed it. Whether or not he was right in his accusations is not something you need to consider; all you need to know is that he held this grudge.

"Another element of the crime that you should be looking at is availability. By that I mean, was the defendant in a location that would have allowed him to do it?

"Here you are limited in that the defense has not mentioned anywhere during the presentation of their case where Mr. Wheeler was when the murder took place. Don't you think they would have told you about it if he was somewhere that could have proven his innocence? If he was on a beach in Aruba, don't you think they would have called a waiter who served him a piña colada that night?

"Next on the list is means; did he have the requisite material and ability to carry out the crime? He certainly had access to the weapon; it wound up in a dumpster a block from his house. And I'm quite sure he had the ability; it doesn't take a trained marksman to fire two bullets into someone's back from a distance of six feet.

"So all the elements of the crime are there and have been demonstrated. Now what else is there for you to consider? To make a fair and reasoned decision, the arguments of both sides must be analyzed.

"It has long been the refuge of guilty parties to claim that while the evidence is overwhelming, the truth is that it's been planted . . . there's been a frame-up! I mean, what else can the defense say?

"You see it all the time, and in recent times it's added a technological element. How many people, when they're caught having sent an improper email, or having posted something unwise and unpleasant on social media, say they've been hacked?

"But in this case, Mr. Carpenter has actually gone a step further than just claiming that there's been a frame-up. He's introduced outside evil figures, people that he has loosely connected to the victim through phone numbers and GPS signals.

"He would have you believe that since the victim knew some bad people, they must have killed him. But did you hear why they would have wanted to do that? Did those bad people threaten him in a restaurant? Was the gun found near their house in a bag filled with their material and DNA?

"We don't know any details about those people or their relationship with Mr. Franklin, or even if they had one at all. All we've heard is where their phones were at various times; we don't even know who was holding those phones at the time.

"I just want to say one other thing, because I think it's

important. There is one person we have not heard much about in this trial, and that is the victim. That is unfortunate. But I'm here to say that Stanley Franklin should be and will be remembered for more than just the way he died.

"He was a husband, a brother, a successful businessman, a philanthropist, and an art collector. He loved beautiful paintings, those of the masters, and he took them into his life, and he gifted them into the lives of others.

"He did not deserve to die in this manner, but there is unfortunately nothing you can do about that. All you can do is get him some measure of justice.

"So please look at the evidence, logically and honestly and without prejudice, and make your decision based on the facts.

"I know you will and that's all I can ask."

No sooner does Dietz's ass hit his seat than I am up and walking toward the jury.

Unlike Dietz, I don't use a lectern or have any notes. I wing it, extemporaneously, though I certainly know the points I'm going to hit.

"Like Mr. Dietz, I would also like to talk about the evidence and ask you to analyze it fairly and objectively. But before I get into that, I'd like to remind you about Jerry Cawley.

"You've heard and seen a lot during this trial, so perhaps you don't remember Mr. Cawley. He is currently in the county jail, but he came out briefly to testify before you. He told you that Jeffrey Wheeler, out of nowhere and for no reason, confessed to him that he murdered Stanley Franklin.

"Now I trust that it was conclusively demonstrated that Cawley was lying; his story made no sense and he could not defend it. Mr. Dietz asked him no questions on redirect to rehabilitate him, which was wise. Cawley was hopelessly compromised. He was here to recount a fairy tale.

"But the crucial issue is not his ridiculous story, but

rather why he came in here to tell it. Mr. Dietz said that his office offered Mr. Cawley nothing in return for his testimony, and I completely and totally believe him. He has far too much integrity for that.

"So who and what prompted Mr. Cawley to come here? There has to be a reason; he must have had something to gain by telling his lies. Someone obviously promised him something; maybe money, maybe something else. Which means that someone was willing to lie and cheat to make sure that Mr. Wheeler gets convicted of this crime.

"Please keep that in mind.

"So now let's get to the evidence. Mr. Wheeler had a grudge against Stanley Franklin; both sides readily admit that. He yelled at him in a restaurant, though while Mr. Dietz called it a threat, no actual threat was made.

"If that grudge and incident in the restaurant were the entirety of the case against Mr. Wheeler, we wouldn't be sitting here. No, we are here because of the plastic bag found in the dumpster a block from Mr. Wheeler's house.

"And, boy, that was some plastic bag. There was a grocery list, a bunch of items with Mr. Wheeler's fingerprints on them, and the murder weapon. It could not have been any more incriminating if it had a neon sign attached to it that screamed, 'I did it! Arrest me!'

"Of course, there were some strange things about that bag. For example, why would someone drive ten miles with something that if discovered could send them to prison, only to throw it away near their house? Aren't there any rivers around that he could have dumped it in?

"And the one thing in the bag that didn't have fingerprints was the murder weapon. Why wipe that clean and place it in a bag with all those other things? Does that make sense?

"Isn't it within reason to believe that it could have been planted? That the plastic bag could have been stolen from Mr. Wheeler's car, the gun placed inside, and then the whole thing dumped near his house? Maybe by the same people who sent Jerry Cawley into this courtroom?

"If they knew about the incident in the restaurant the night before, wouldn't that have made Mr. Wheeler an ideal patsy?

"You also saw a great deal of evidence, phone and GPS records. Mr. Dietz disparages such evidence, but there is one thing absolutely true about it: it cannot be planted or faked.

"And what does it show? It chronicles the phone calls and movements of Nick Edwards, a career criminal, and Tony Bradley, a cop killer. It connects them by phone to the victim in this case, Stanley Franklin.

"And not only that, it places them within a few blocks of the murder scene, Mr. Franklin's house, around the time of the shooting. What were they doing there?

"I can't prove that Tony Bradley killed Stanley Franklin any more than Mr. Dietz can prove that Jeffrey Wheeler did. But isn't it entirely possible that Bradley did it? Bradley is a murderer; Jeffrey Wheeler was never so much as accused of a crime in his life.

"Your job, as Judge Eddings will no doubt explain, is not to solve a murder. You are not investigators; you are the triers of fact. It is to determine whether the accused, in this case Jeffrey Wheeler, committed this crime beyond a reasonable doubt.

"I would submit that reasonable doubt is all over this case; it permeates every inch of it. I hope and trust you will feel the same way and give Jeffrey Wheeler his life back.

"He has suffered enough, starting with the loss of the love of his life, and continuing right up until this moment. Thank you."

It's been two days since the jury was given their charge by Judge Eddings and sent out to deliberate.

During that time I've bounced around a lot in my view of how it is going to turn out. On the first day I thought we'd lose in one day. On the second day, I thought we'd lose in two days.

Now that two days are in the book, I'm pretty sure we'll lose on the third day. As you might be able to tell, I'm not feeling too upbeat.

What I'm hoping for is a hung jury. I don't usually root for that as a result, but I don't think all twelve jury members are going to find our arguments more compelling than that goddamn bag in the dumpster.

If the jury is hung, I'm sure the case will be retried, which would likely mean that Jeff would stay in jail until then. But it would give us a chance to investigate more and maybe solve the problems we have so far been unable to solve.

While waiting for a verdict I always feel like one large, raw, exposed nerve ending, which is not the most comfortable feeling in the world. For the sake of those around me, I try to act normally, but when I told that to Laurie, she said that in my case normal is not necessarily something to aspire to.

The dogs have been a source of some comfort, and our walks have been frequent and long. Of course, seeing Rufus bothers me a bit because it makes me remember that his owner, the person who saved his life, is languishing in a jail cell.

His innocent owner.

I've visited Jeff twice and he is appropriately nervous. He thinks we're going to win, and while I don't argue the opposite, nor do I agree with him. The furthest I will go is to say that juries are unpredictable.

I've also visited the Tara Foundation a couple of times, but the problem with that is Willie keeps telling me how positive he is that I am going to win. I got Willie off on appeal after he spent seven years in prison for a murder he did not commit, so he pretty much thinks I walk on legal water.

Tonight Laurie, Ricky, and I are out to dinner. Laurie suggested a barbecue restaurant because she knows my mental state is too fragile to deal with sushi. Ricky's fine with it; he'll pretty much eat anything, even vegetables.

My son eats vegetables. . . . I find it hard to come to terms with that. I've been assuming for years that he will outgrow it, but it doesn't seem like it's going to happen. But it still pains me when the waiter comes over and Ricky asks how they prepare the brussels sprouts.

I try not to talk about the case, and I'm mostly successful in that regard. But I do mention that the auction is going to be held in five days, and that the speculation in the press is that it could go as high as $250 million.

"For some paintings?" Ricky asks when he finishes chewing the brussels sprouts. He's obviously incredulous at the amount.

"Yes," Laurie says.

"For real?" he asks, and that gets me to thinking. I'm quiet for a while, since I can't think, talk, and chew at the same time, and Laurie asks me if something is wrong.

"Ricky just asked if it was for real, and Willie Miller had asked me the same thing. I know they were talking about the price, but maybe the question better applies to the paintings themselves."

"What do you mean?"

"What if they are fakes? Forgeries? How do we know for sure that they're real?"

"We've discussed this before, Andy. They've been verified as genuine by two sets of experts, and then by the Metropolitan Museum of Art."

"I know. But what if they found a way around it? It would clear up one question at the very least."

"What's that?"

"Well, maybe the paintings lost in the explosion were also fake. Then Franklin, a lover of art, wouldn't have minded losing them. He would have been happy to take the insurance money."

"I'm not buying it, Andy."

"I'm not selling it. At least not yet."

"So where can you go with this? And at the end of the day, what does it have to do with your case?"

"I don't know the answer to either of those questions. But I'm going to find out whatever I can."

"How?"

"I don't know that either."

Laurie smiles. "Let me know if I can help."

I take the dogs for a walk when I get home to decide how to approach this.

The dogs are no help, in fact they represent the opposite of what I am talking about. Everything to them is real, every walk, every smell, every biscuit.

They live entirely in the real world and are not in the slightest way deceptive. They let you know when they want something, when they're frightened, when they're happy, when they're whatever. There is absolutely nothing fake about them.

Humans are different; there is plenty fake about them. It's not always intended negatively; even the grass we're walking on might be artificial if an NFL game was going to be played on it.

But when money is involved, deceit is always a possibility, and there is plenty of money to be made in this auction. I have no idea if my hypothesis is correct, but it gives me something to do and think about while I agonize over the verdict.

Even if I am correct, I agree with Laurie that it's not necessarily going to be helpful to my case. That's true for two reasons. One is that it doesn't clear up why Tony Bradley killed Stanley Franklin. And two, our case is over.

Technically, if new and compelling evidence were to come up, it would be possible to reopen the evidentiary portion of the trial. But that is a steep hill to climb, and there is no way it can happen before the jury finishes their work. And once a verdict is delivered, the legal ship has sailed. The only thing left would be a lengthy appeal.

By the time we get home, I've come up with a plan, pathetic and weak as it is. I'm going to start by researching whatever I can about previous known forgeries of fine art, as well as the process for verification.

It ain't much, but it's all I got.

My first call will be to Robby Divine, but it's getting late so that will have to wait until the morning. The other thing I will do is google whatever I can about the subject, and that's something I will tackle tomorrow as well.

For now I'll just read through the discovery for the umpteenth time until it reveals something to me or puts me to sleep. The latter is more likely.

I jump around and wind up with the financial records of Marstan that Sam provided. They're obviously endless; it's a big company. But Sam has done excellent summaries for me, telling me what they've been spending their money on. He also pointed out anything that he felt was unusual.

I don't find anything that he listed to be unusual at all, but what I do find interesting is something that's not here. It's possible Sam missed it, but Sam is not the miss-it type.

It's never too late to call Sam; I don't think he ever sleeps. Or maybe he's on cybertime, which earthlings like me don't understand. But he answers on the first ring as always, with no sign of sleepiness in his voice.

I ask him about the issue I discovered, or more properly didn't discover, and he confirms it's not there. "I can't believe I didn't notice that," he says.

I wouldn't say I'm excited, but I am intrigued. I go upstairs to the bedroom and Laurie is asleep. I don't want to wake her for this, but I really want to tell her.

So I make as much noise as I can and flick the lights on and off a few times. I scream in pain pretending that I stubbed my toe. I'm putting on quite a performance, but she sleeps through it. Maybe I should feel for a pulse.

Finally, she stirs. "Andy, what the hell are you doing?"

"Trying to wake you. It wasn't easy."

"Here's another approach, just for future reference. You could gently touch me and say, 'Honey, I need you to wake up.'"

"I never considered that."

"Why do you want me up?"

"I was looking through Franklin's and his company's financial records. He said at the initial press conference that it cost them a fortune to find and acquire these paintings. He said it ran into eight figures."

"So?"

"So it's horseshit. According to Sam and these records, he never spent a dime."

As always, Robby Divine was totally and immediately helpful.

Robby is one of the wealthiest men in the world; he owns part or all of seemingly every business in the country. But his real business appears to be making money, and he does it 24-7.

We met at a charity dinner once and became sort of friends. We have an interesting relationship: he does me favors and in return I tell him that his beloved Chicago Cubs are not horrible. He knows I'm lying but appears to appreciate the effort.

I also went to a charity event he sponsored at the Metropolitan Museum of Art, so I thought he might know people in that world. I was right, mainly because he knows people in every world.

I asked if he could connect me with someone who could give me a quick course for dummies in fine art and potential forgery of said fine art. That's why I am sitting with Victor Ivey, a former curator at the Whitney.

We're meeting at his brownstone on Seventy-seventh Street off Columbus in Manhattan, which is risky for me. I need to be on call for a verdict and am required to be at the court within an hour if necessary. If I get the call while I'm here, an hour is not going to do it.

On the way here I had called Captain Hornstein of the Paramus Fire Department. I'm sure he's already spent much more time on this case than he'd like, but he's been patient and helpful, so I figured I'd give it another shot.

"Captain, I asked you this once before, but I'd like to press you on it. Do you know for a fact that the paintings were in that studio when the explosion and fire happened?"

"A fact? I could never say that, but the insurance company didn't question it, and I saw damaged paintings there."

"You did? You didn't say that before."

"I had meant that I had no idea if they were the same paintings that Franklin claimed they were. But I saw paintings; they were certainly ruined but not totally destroyed. And I was there when the insurance people arrived. I had to escort them in to check the damage. No, there were definitely paintings there."

I thanked him and got off the phone. . . . Another theory had been eliminated and my forgery theory remained intact, though barely.

Very often people don't look and act like their occupations, but Victor Ivey certainly does. He is refined and dignified and speaks softly and precisely. I would have guessed college English literature professor, but museum curator fits perfectly.

I tell Ivey about my potential timing conflict, so we get right to it. I decide to be direct. "I'm trying to gauge the potential for the paintings that are about to be auctioned at the Echelon to be forgeries."

He doesn't look shocked; I don't think "shocked" is part of his repertoire. But he simply says, "Good luck with that."

"So not possible?"

"I would never say that anything I do not have personal knowledge of is impossible, but it is extremely unlikely. It is my understanding that two sets of experts, as well as technicians from the Met, have examined the works and certified them as real."

"How do paintings get certified?"

"There are basically two ways. One is human; there are people who are experts in the field who analyze the work and render a judgment. These people are very good at what they do; they have devoted their lives to it."

"And the second way?"

"Radioactive carbon dating. How technical do you want me to get?"

"Moderately."

"Fine. It measures the amount of carbon-fourteen. All material contains it but loses it over time. By measuring how much is left, one can tell how old something is."

"They test the painting itself?"

"Not often. Usually it's done on the canvas; if a canvas dates back to 1500, it's unlikely the painting on it was done last Wednesday. In many cases, small pieces of the art itself can be tested, provided it can be done without damaging the work. I would think at least one set of experts did that in this case, but I obviously can't be sure."

"What about the players involved here? Stanley Franklin, when he was alive, and the people at Echelon."

"Excellent reputations. I've known Wallace Linder for years. I never met Stanley, but he was known as a true lover of fine art. And very knowledgeable as well. These are men who would be very difficult to fool."

"Has it ever happened? Have people this knowledgeable and well thought of been fooled?"

"Oh, yes, but rarely. There was a famous case with the Knoedler Gallery right here in Manhattan. Like I say, it's rare, but then again it could possibly happen more frequently and remain undiscovered. After all, the goal of the forgers is to remain undiscovered."

As I'm ready to leave, I thank him for his time, and he says, "My pleasure. It was also nice to hear from Robby, we haven't spoken in well over a year. Our relationship has become somewhat contentious over time."

I'm surprised to hear this, and I ask if he would tell me why.

"I'm a St. Louis Cardinals fan."

I nod. "Enough said."

I'm driving home and on Route Four in Paramus when Eddie Dowd calls me. I know what he's going to say before he says it.

"The jury is back. They want us down there."

"Is there a verdict?"

"I don't know."

There are three possibilities for what might take place in a few minutes.

One is that the jury will announce that they have reached a verdict, and they will reveal it. The second is that they will say they are deadlocked, in which case it is overwhelmingly likely that the judge will send them back to try again. The third possibility is that they have questions or want something read back to them.

In all cases the lawyers need to be present, so here we are.

Before Judge Eddings comes in, Dietz starts walking toward me. I get up to meet him halfway; I'm not sure I want Jeff to hear what he has to say before I hear it.

"I think they're deadlocked," he says.

"Wouldn't surprise me." That is true because nothing would surprise me other than an outright acquittal.

I'm fairly positive that Dietz is going to be correct. He would have more access to inside information than I would, but he would also not tell me his view unless he was at least mostly sure he was right. Lawyers never like to be shown to be wrong in settings like this; he wouldn't have volunteered his prediction unless he knew he was going to be proven correct.

I go back to the defense table and share with Jeff and Eddie what Dietz said.

"Is that good news?" Jeff asks.

"It depends what the count is."

"Are they going to announce that?"

"No."

Judge Eddings finally comes in and calls in the jury. I can't tell from their expressions what is happening, but we're going to know very soon.

Eddings calls on the foreman, who confirms that they are deadlocked and unable to reach a verdict.

"I understand this is very difficult," the judge says. "But very often in these situations further efforts bear fruit. So I am going to send you back to continue your deliberations and ask you to do your utmost to come to a decision."

And that's it. The jurors trudge back to the jury room, the judge adjourns the session, and the media and other onlookers in the gallery sag with disappointment. Nobody likes waiting.

Least of all me.

"I don't know how they could have done it," I say to Laurie.

We're having a glass of wine in the den; Ricky is in his room probably pretending to do his homework. I've heard him yell, "Oh, come on," a couple of times, which means his math assignment has taken a negative turn, or his Madden football team just got scored on.

"You're still talking about the paintings being forged?" Laurie asks.

"Yes. I've been googling and reading as much as I can about it online. I can't figure out how they did it."

"Maybe they didn't do it."

"Always possible. But I can't think of any other reason Franklin would have allowed the pieces in the office to get destroyed. He could have moved them out weeks before the explosion without attracting suspicion. And the fact that Franklin lied about spending all that money on the hunt for this artwork supports my theory."

"Maybe he was just trying to sound more heroic and self-sacrificing. Maybe he got lucky and the paintings fell into his lap."

"Or maybe they're forged."

"Andy, you're just not in a position to know. Which is okay, because even if you did know, it does nothing for your case. Which is also okay, because your case is over anyway. You even said that."

"All true. But the idea of these people committing murder and then getting rich in the process is driving me a bit crazy."

"You're always crazy when you're waiting for a verdict."

"Then crazier." Then, "Did you know that there was an art gallery in the city, called Knoedler, which was the center of a big scandal? They bought and sold all kinds of forged paintings, allegedly by famous people, without even knowing it."

"How did that happen?"

"There are these people, they can paint and copy anything. They can reproduce the great works and make them look absolutely real."

"I didn't know that."

"So if a guy can paint exactly like da Vinci, copy it so well that you think it's an original, is he as talented as da Vinci? Is he as great an artist?"

"No. I don't think so," Laurie says. "Da Vinci had the vision and imagination."

"Like the *Mona Lisa*? Did it take vision and imagination to paint a face?"

"Books have been written about that painting. Next time you're googling, look up the golden ratio."

"I don't get it; Mona is not even that good-looking."

"It's possible you have some limitations intellectually," Laurie says, smiling.

"You're not the first person to tell me that."

"So what are you going to do about your forgery theory? I've got a hunch you're not going to drop it."

"That's for damn sure."

"Who do you think is behind it?"

"The people who stand to profit from it. Margaret Franklin and Wilson Paul."

Wilson Paul didn't want to meet with me again. It's a shocker, but I don't think he likes me.

He relented when I told him on the phone that it was literally a matter of life and death. I think that piqued his curiosity.

He told me he'd give me ten minutes; I assume that's five for life and five for death.

Once I'm seated in his office, he glares at me. "Life and death, huh?"

I shrug. "You think that was over-the-top?"

"What the hell do you want?"

"I'm sensing some hostility here. I didn't call you to testify; I thought that would make us buddies."

"If you had called me, your boy would have been convicted already. So I repeat, what the hell do you want?"

"I just wanted to tell you that I know about the forgeries."

He looks a bit stunned for a moment, or maybe that's just my imagination.

"What are you talking about?"

"I'm talking about the paintings being auctioned off. They're fakes."

He frowns derisively. "Is that right? They're been verified by three sets of experts and carbon-dated, but ambulance chaser Andy Carpenter says they're fakes?"

I nod. "Yes, he does. And he's going to expose you and send you to a real jail. Unless you're willing to share in the profits."

"Is that right?"

"Yes. We ambulance chasers see art forgery as a victimless crime. The purchaser wants the status and wants to hang the thing on his wall and brag to his friends. He can do that whether the stuff is real or not. It's a win-win for the seller and buyer."

"Interesting. Now get out of my office."

"Happy to. You've got forty-eight hours to agree to my sharing proposals; otherwise I will blow your scheme right out of the water."

I have no idea if I'm right about any of this.

I'm probably not because I cannot understand how they could have fooled all those experts and the scientific testing. But it's still the only thing that makes sense . . . sort of.

I'm also very possibly wrong about Wilson Paul being involved. But he benefited from Franklin's death; he moved to the top rung of the business and got the fancy office. He also has a piece of the action, so whatever his portion is, if the art sells for hundreds of millions, he stands to make a nice piece of change.

My sense was that behind his bluster he was worried about what I had to say. That may or may not be true, but my goal was not to get him to blurt out a confession in his office. It was to make him panic and make a mistake.

Laurie thinks that if I'm right, they will come after me, and she doesn't mean to share the money. I doubt that's the case because the resulting publicity could be devastating for them. The last thing they want is more attention on Franklin's death and Jeff's trial. They might also think that I've discussed my theory with others, who would come forward if I was attacked or worse.

But maybe she's right, and if she is, hopefully she has Marcus nearby. I haven't come out and asked her, but maybe I will. For now I want to pretend I'm manly.

If nothing else, I am accomplishing one thing by pursuing this theory: I am distracting myself from the agony of waiting for the verdict. Of course, that's not entirely true; I'm thinking about the jury every minute of every day. But this way I also have something else on my mind.

We're now in the fourth day, and there has been continued silence from the jury. No questions, no requests for read backs, no pleas to be let out of their deliberation prison . . . nothing.

The auction is in just a few days. There has been a great deal of coverage in the media about it. I think that the paintings were said to have been stolen and hidden by the Nazis makes for a more interesting story than just some dry artwork sales. It's not the Super Bowl, but it has captured at least some public interest.

The auction is going to be live streamed; pretty much everything is live streamed these days. I would expect that soon America and the world will be able to watch me walk Tara and Hunter in Eastside Park. It would make for riveting television.

So now I am waiting on Wilson Paul, and waiting on the auction, and waiting on a verdict.

Did I mention that I hate waiting?

I'm hoping that this is my last case for a while, and by *while* I mean many decades.

I've given up calling myself retired; maybe the way to do it is to pretend I'm still working while not taking on any cases. That would be a de facto retirement, which is almost as good as the real thing.

Of course, this case could conceivably go on for a long time. If the jury is hung, I'm sure that in a case this high profile it would be retried. That would add months to the process, even if it's done quickly.

If it turned out that the jury was leaning toward acquittal, there is always a chance that the judge would reconsider and allow bail while we waited for the new trial. Not to do so would in effect be sentencing Jeff to a long term in jail . . . presumption of innocence be damned.

Bail would obviously make Jeff's life more livable and ease the pressure on his lawyer.

I'm closing up the office today, which just means putting away some files. Edna's area obviously needs no tidying up; it's not like she spent any time here. Any typing she does for Eddie she does at home, and he corrects the numerous errors at his home.

Sam is in his office when I get here, so I stop in to say hello. He asks how the verdict wait is going.

"I don't know how to answer that, Sam. Nothing happens until it happens; and then it's too late."

"You're going to win."

"Why do you say that?"

"Because I can't picture you losing."

I guess I should take that as a compliment, but it doesn't make me any more confident. For one thing, Sam did not see one minute of the trial. For another, I can picture me losing.

I can also picture Jeff going to jail for the rest of his life, and Margaret Franklin and Wilson Paul getting away with murder and walking away with $200 million. That picture scares the hell out of me.

Of course, the truth is I don't know for certain that Margaret Franklin and Wilson Paul murdered Stanley Franklin. But someone hired Bradley, and those two make the most sense, since they will make the most money from Franklin's death.

Margaret's former close friend Melinda Seeley said that she was sure Margaret was having an affair. Maybe it was with Paul, which would add another layer to their motive.

I go back to my office to put the files away. I look out the window at Van Houten Street; there's a check-cashing business, a bodega, and a gas station across the street. Then below me I can see the awning over the fruit stand.

This is the big time.

I'm almost finished when I hear a commotion out in the hall. I open the door and see two men squaring off as if to fight. A gun is lying on the floor down toward Sam's office.

One of the men is huge, maybe six-four and 250 pounds with a chest that looks like someone could go over Niagara Falls in it. The other man is Marcus.

I move along the wall down toward the gun and pick it up. Now I have it, but I have no idea what I'll do with it.

Meanwhile, Marcus is taking this guy seriously. I haven't run into many worthy adversaries for Marcus in a while and it scares me. Fortunately, it doesn't seem to scare Marcus.

The intruder throws a punch that hits Marcus in the upper shoulder and moves him a step back. Then he does it again, and Marcus is moved another step back, now getting closer to the stairway.

I've never seen this before. Usually by this stage of a fight Marcus is the only one still conscious. But the intruder's punches are short and lightning fast, like pistons, and Marcus has not adjusted to it. It looks like he's trying to figure out the best way to deal with this threat.

The guy throws a third punch, and three turns out not to be a charm. Marcus catches the guy's fist with his bare hand and in one motion redirects it and slams it into the wall with incredible power. The guy screams; he must have more broken fingers than he has fingers.

He lashes out with his remaining hand, and Marcus does exactly the same thing with that one. It hits the wall with a deafening crash, which is partially drowned out by more screams of pain. If anyone is downstairs buying bananas, I can't imagine what they're thinking.

Unless the intruder has an extra one in his pocket, he is effectively out of hands. So he kicks at Marcus, screaming all the time. Marcus does something that I wish I could have video recorded because no one will believe it possible.

He grabs the guy's leg and swings him like he's throwing a discus. But he doesn't throw him against the wall, he throws him down the stairs.

Until now, if I thought about someone falling down a flight of stairs, I would visualize that person stumbling and rolling, hitting each stair as he falls.

Not this time. The human discus doesn't hit a stair until he is three away from the bottom. I do a quick count and realize he had flown over the first eleven stairs, face-planting on stair three. That has to be some kind of stair-flying record.

"Holy shit," Sam says, having joined me and Marcus at the top of the stairs as we look down at the intruder, clearly out cold. Then, to Marcus, "How the hell did you do that?"

Marcus does not respond because he is Marcus.

I realize I still have the gun in my hand and I put it down carefully on the floor. "Sam, can you call nine one one?"

"Yeah . . . sure. What should I tell them?"

"That we have an armed intruder, but that we subdued him."

Sam looks down at the guy again. "We sure did."

The officers respond to the call remarkably quickly; they are here in less than five minutes.

For the intruder lying on the steps, it might as well be five years, because he has taken his last stair flight. Apparently the impact crushed the front of his skull, and the arriving officers cannot find a pulse.

If he has left any message at all in death, it is "You kids, don't try this at home. Take one stair at a time."

Marcus, Sam, and I are kept upstairs while the first responders and coroner's people deal with the guy's body. They've closed down the fruit stand and moved everybody out.

I can't imagine my landlady and owner of the stand, Sofia Hernandez, is going to be pleased. I think I'm going to unilaterally give myself a rent increase.

Two homicide detectives question us, separately, in my office. I don't envy them having to interview Marcus; they should get Laurie down here to be their interpreter.

I call Laurie and tell her what happened and she does come down, though she is not allowed to talk to us until the interviews are over. Pete Stanton arrives as well; he comes in when I'm in Sam's office having just signed a statement.

"So, just another day at the office?" Pete asks.

"Pretty much. But I'm getting a lot done . . . writing reports, dictating memos . . ."

"You want to tell me why the coroner just peeled a body off your staircase?"

"Sure. He tried to kill me. Marcus, who was in the neighborhood, stopped him. The guy then thought better of it and left by way of the staircase."

"Does this have anything to do with your case?"

"You know what? I think I'm going to try something different and answer that honestly. But first tell me who the hell he is."

Pete nods. "Fair enough. His name is Eddie Squires; he's a known associate of Tony Bradley and was also wanted for murder in two jurisdictions. Those jurisdictions will probably be pleased by today's event."

"So we performed a public service."

"You'll get a key to the city. Now what, if anything, does this have to do with your case?"

Usually I offer as little information as possible, but in this case I don't see any harm, and possibly some benefit, in the authorities knowing what is going on. "You know who Wilson Paul is?"

"No," Pete says. "Enlighten me. But first tell me, did you tell my people any of what you're about to say when they questioned you just now?"

"No, I gave them a lot of word-salad bullshit."

He nods. "Figures. Now tell me about Wilson Paul."

"He's a minority partner in Marstan Industries and is now running the company by himself after Stanley Franklin's death."

"What does he have to do with this?"

"I threatened him a few days ago, and I believe this was his response to my threat."

"Threatened him how?"

"We're now moving into my theories, okay? I can't prove any of what I am going to tell you."

Pete frowns. "What else is new?"

"Did you read about the artwork Franklin got . . . supposedly the Nazis hid it . . . that's going up for auction in the city? It's going to get bids in nine figures."

"Yeah. I should have been a painter."

"Well, I think they're fake. Forgeries."

"Doesn't that stuff get checked out?"

"Totally and completely. But I think they found a way around it. It doesn't matter why I think that, but what just happened makes me more positive that I'm right. My threat to Paul was that I would expose the forgeries. He sent the Flying Wallenda to stop me."

"Why was Marcus here?" Pete asks.

"Because we anticipated this. There's a lot of money at stake here. Even more than the tab at Charlie's . . . though not by much."

"The forensics people said there were no signs Squires hit any steps on the way down; no blood, no hair, nothing."

"It was thrilling to watch."

"So if you're right about the forgeries, and about this

Paul guy . . . I guess there's a first time for everything . . . but if you're right, how can I help?"

"I don't know. I don't know how to expose any of this because I don't know how it's done. I don't know how all those experts can be wrong. Even the Metropolitan Museum checked out the works, and they don't stand to profit from any of them. And I don't even have any way to prove that the dead guy on stair three is connected to any of it."

"So what can I do?"

"For now? Tell your people to take as much fruit as they want from downstairs. Just tell Sofia that I'm going to pay for all of it. I need to make this up to her."

"I can do that," Pete says.

For me, this is as frustrating as it gets.

There is a great deal that I know, or at least I think I know. I know that Tony Bradley killed Stanley Franklin. I know that it was at the behest of Wilson Paul and most probably Margaret Franklin as well.

Now that Paul sent Squires after me as a result of my threatening exposure of the forgery plot, I know that I was right; the paintings are somehow fake. They have to be.

I know that the explosion at Marstan was deliberate, and that Tony Bradley was involved. I know that the paintings destroyed in the blast must also have been fake, and that their destruction was designed to get the insurance money.

The frustrating part is that I can't do anything about any of it. I can't prove the conspiracy involving Margaret Franklin and Wilson Paul. I can't prove that Bradley and Squires were working for them, or that Bradley pulled the trigger.

Just as important, I can't prove that the paintings are fake. I am powerless to make anyone else believe it. My publicly saying it would easily be refuted, since so much time and effort have gone into verifying their authenticity.

I would sound like a raving maniac, and my claims would easily be discounted.

Of course, there's also a lot that I don't know. I don't know why Stanley Franklin was killed, since he was obviously a crucial part of the conspiracy. I don't know why the building explosion happened while people were present, though it's possible it was to prevent them from revealing what they had discovered about Franklin.

I'm feeling a lot of pressure to do something about all of this. That pressure will increase tenfold if Jeff is found guilty, because I will have to prepare an appeal. Surely uncovering the conspiracy would be crucial in that effort, since it would include the revelation of who had ordered Bradley to pull the trigger.

The last thing I don't know, and this has been true for a long time, is why the hell I went to law school.

This time the call from the court clerk comes to me.

The clerk's name is Rita Gordon and we have a bit of a history together. Laurie and I had broken up once well before we reunited and were married; she had moved back to her hometown in Wisconsin.

Rita and I had a brief affair, and by brief I mean that it lasted for about forty-five minutes. But they were forty-five great minutes, and we have remained friends ever since.

"Andy, you need to get down here. The jury is coming back in."

"Are they hung?" I ask, fully expecting that the answer will be yes.

"No, there's a verdict."

There is a thumping noise, and I'm about to ask Rita what it was when I realize that it was the sound of my heart hitting the floor. A verdict is the last thing I want.

"I'll be there," I say because I don't have a choice.

When I hang up, I see Laurie standing in the doorway. "They've reached a verdict?"

"I'm afraid so."

"Are you just being pessimistic, or do you really think you lost?"

"Both."

"I'll go with you. You shouldn't drive in this condition."

We get to the courthouse around forty minutes after Rita's call, and the place is already packed and buzzing. I don't know how that happened, unless these people were camping out on the front steps of the courthouse.

Eddie Dowd is at the defense table when I get inside, and Dietz and his people are here as well. Dietz and I make eye contact, and he gives me a small nod. I think it's meant to show respect, and a kinship that comes from having been in this battle, but I don't know. And I don't care.

If we lose, I'm going to hate everyone that's been involved in this case, starting with the jury. Dietz will be on that hate list, so I might as well start now.

Jeff is brought into the courtroom and takes his seat between me and Eddie. "Do we think they're still hung?"

I think Jeff has gone from dreading a hung jury to hoping for one, if for no reason than to avoid the finality of a guilty verdict. I have the exact same feeling.

"No, there's a verdict."

I try to replay the facts of the case in my head, weighing the evidence on both sides. But the effort is exhausting, and totally and completely unproductive. It no longer matters what I think and hasn't for a while.

Jeff's fate is in the hands of twelve fine citizens, or twelve total assholes. I can let you know which in a few minutes.

Judge Eddings is late coming into the courtroom. I

cannot imagine what she could be doing that is more important than this. Maybe she just wants to make a grand entrance, but if she doesn't hurry up, I am going to go into her chambers and drag her out here by her robe.

Finally she arrives and the entire place goes silent. There is not an empty seat in the gallery and people are standing in the back. It feels like there is a pent-up energy and when the cap is taken off the bottle, it will explode.

I think Judge Eddings realizes this because she spends an inordinate amount of time warning everyone against an outburst when the verdict is read. Good luck with that.

Finally, after what seems like a month, she calls in the jury. They do not look at the defense table when they are brought in, which is never a good sign. Or maybe it is; I have no idea. At least they don't look at Dietz either.

Eddings asks the foreperson, a woman, if they have reached a verdict and she confirms that they have. Eddings asks her to give the verdict sheet to the clerk, who in turn brings it to the judge, who reads it, expressionless.

I don't know why judges have to get an advance look and thus delay things; it's always bugged me. I've never seen them change anything; they just give it back to be read. Maybe it gives them a feeling of superiority to be the only person in the place, besides the jury, who knows how this will play out.

"Will the defendant please stand," Eddings says.

Jeff, Eddie, and I rise as one. I have my hand on Jeff's left shoulder and Eddie has his hand on Jeff's right shoulder. In Eddie's case it's to offer comfort and support; in my case it's to keep me upright on legs that feel like jelly.

I don't know how Jeff is able to stand the pressure. If the verdict is guilty, Eddie and I will be crushed, but we'll be able to go home and come to terms with it. I'll love my family and walk my dogs and watch football and basketball. Jeff's life will effectively be over, at least in any form that he'd want to live it.

"Read the verdict, please," Eddings says to the clerk, so she does. I briefly wonder if she is nervous; then I realize that I don't care. I just want to get this over with.

"'We the jury, in the case of the *State of New Jersey versus Jeffrey Wheeler*, find the defendant, Jeffrey Wheeler, as it relates to the charge of murder in the first degree of Stanley Franklin, not guilty.'"

The gallery explodes and Judge Eddings starts pounding her gavel, demanding order in her courtroom. I'm finding it hard to catch my breath, a situation made worse by Jeff hugging me so hard that he's compressing my lungs.

Finally he turns and hugs Eddie, and I find that I have to sit down and get control of myself. These moments are getting way too stressful for me.

Dietz asks for the jury to be polled, and all twelve of these beautiful, wonderful, extraordinary people confirm their not-guilty votes. I don't know how many of them had been on the other side, only finally to be convinced after such a long time. It doesn't matter; the good guys were obviously persuasive.

Laurie is in the gallery, and when I catch her eye, she gives me two thumbs up. I'm sure she is thrilled for Jeff and maybe just as thrilled not to have to deal with my personality and attitude if we had lost. I can be slightly annoying, or so I'm told. I don't see it.

Judge Eddings thanks the jury and adjourns the session. Dietz comes over to congratulate me and shake my hand, both of which I appreciate. I'm sure he noticed that my hand is still shaking.

I wait while Jeff goes off to fill out some paperwork and then comes back to the table. "Let's go," I say. "Laurie and I will drive you home."

"I can go now? Just like that?"

"Just like that. Let's blow this pop stand."

Laurie and I drop Jeff off at his house.

He's surprisingly quiet on the way; it's hard to imagine the emotions he must be feeling. There was a damn good chance he would never see that house again. In fact, when he gets out of the car, he stares at it for maybe fifteen seconds, trying to take it in.

Once he's out of the car, Laurie says, "You did it, Andy. You're amazing."

"I cannot go through this again."

"You always say that."

"And I always mean it, but this time more than most. I thought I was going to pass out waiting for that verdict."

"Remember what you said to me when this whole thing started?"

"Was it some complaint about missing NFL playoff games?"

"No. You said that you were a lawyer. That there was no sense denying it."

"Did you really have to remember that and repeat it back to me? What are you, a court stenographer?"

She laughs. "No, I'm an ex-cop and investigator. And you are a lawyer. Deal with it."

"Maybe I just need some guilty clients; some cold-blooded murderers. Then I won't be so afraid I'm going to lose."

We get home and give Rufus the good news. It's sort of bittersweet; he's become good friends with Tara and Hunter. Even Sebastian, in those rare moments when he's awake and moving around the house, seems to like Rufus.

We do a biscuit celebration, and about an hour later Jeff arrives. Rufus goes absolutely nuts when he sees him, and it's beautiful to watch. I'm sure Rufus doesn't remember Jeff rescuing him from the burning building; he just knows that it's someone he loves.

Jeff stays for a while until I start getting uncomfortable with the repeated *Thank you*s, and I suggest he take Rufus home and reacquaint him with his surroundings. We give Jeff some of Rufus's food and a bunch of the toys he has shown a liking for, and they're off.

I'm feeling unusually good until I see a small piece on the news about the auction at Echelon tomorrow. Suddenly I'm aggravated again, which is in a way comforting, since it's my natural state of being.

I can't stand the idea that the conspirators are going to get away with everything, including murder. I still believe that the paintings are forgeries, though I am fully aware that no one would believe me if I proclaimed it to the world.

Maybe the most distressing thing of all is that Wilson Paul, after trying to have me killed for threatening him, is going to laugh all the way to the bank. He knows that

I know, and he's going to see that there's nothing I can do about it.

Once the bidding is over, I intend to privately convey my concerns to whoever is the purchaser. Then it will be up to him or her to believe me or not, and to investigate or not.

The weird thing, at least in my mind, is that to the new owner the legitimacy of the pieces might not even matter. They are apparently just as beautiful as if painted by the masters, so he or she can happily stare at them to their heart's content. That person can brag and show off as if they have the originals because everyone will think it's true.

But I will know better, and the knowledge of that might well drive me crazy. The way I'm feeling now, it will be a short drive.

I take the dogs for my first walk as a lawyer without a case.

It's an incredibly freeing feeling; my mind can now be open and available to focus on the important things in life, like the upcoming NCAA basketball tournament.

I have thought about case strategy 24-7 for a long time now and it is wonderful to get it behind me. I still can't believe that we won, though in retrospect I think the jury made the right call.

I doubt that they fully believe that Jeff is innocent. But with all the connections I made between Bradley, Edwards, and Stanley Franklin, especially Bradley's and Edwards's presence in Alpine at the time of the murders, reasonable doubt had to have kicked in.

An article in the paper today said when the jury originally said they were hung, the vote was 8–4 for acquittal. I'm surprised we did that well that quickly.

We're just entering the park. I have no idea if Marcus is still looking out for me, but it's certainly not necessary if he is. For one thing, the conspirators have lost Edwards, Bradley, and now Squires; they may well have run out of thugs.

But there is no longer any reason to silence me; I've lost in my bid to throw off the auction, and the bad guys have won. The trial is over and the media will move on. I'm clearly not a threat to them anymore, so why stir up more trouble?

The auction is tomorrow at 3:00 P.M. and I am going to try to be doing something else then. I just don't want to see it; it will be too annoying. I'll definitely hear about it after the fact, and I'll attempt to warn the buyer, though they probably won't pay attention.

Even in the unlikely event that the paintings are not forgeries, I find it amazing that someone will pay the kind of money that is expected. "Tara, they're going to make hundreds of millions of dollars."

Tara seems unimpressed; money has never been important to her. Give her biscuits and a warm bed and she is happy with the world. Hunter feels the same way, and even Sebastian as well.

"How can they be worth that much?" I ask, but Tara just keeps sniffing the ground.

Then I remember something that Sam said to me: "Art is really only worth what people will pay for it."

And then it all clicks into place.

"Guys, I'm sorry, but we need to cut the walk short."

"**S**am, I need you to do two things for me, and doing them immediately is not soon enough."

I called Sam the moment I got back into the house and took the leashes off.

"I'm ready." One thing is true of Sam: he's always ready.

"There must be an insurance policy on the art that is going to be auctioned. It must have originally been taken out by Stanley Franklin and probably now reverts to Margaret as the beneficiary."

"What about it?"

"I need to know the terms. By that I mean what it's valued at. What the insurance company has to pay if something happens to the paintings."

"Okay. It's a big number, I'm sure. Might be multiple companies."

"Fine, doesn't matter. I just want to know the number. And if there isn't a number, especially if there isn't a number, I want to know that too. You might be able to find the contract sitting in the Marstan computers."

"No problem. Anything else?"

"Yes. I need you to do another GPS track on a phone."

I tell Sam the phone I need tracked and I let him off the call to do his thing.

My next call is to Pete Stanton. "Pete, you asked how you can help me."

"It was a weak moment. I have no interest in helping you."

"How about if it will make you a hero?"

"On the other hand, what are friends for?"

"It's beautiful that we're able to share this moment. What connections do you have with NYPD?"

"Plenty. We've worked together a few times."

"Excellent." I tell Pete what I need and send him off to renew those connections.

My last call is to Robby Divine to ask for yet another favor. "What is it this time? You want to meet with the president?"

"No, but close. I want to talk to someone at the Metropolitan Museum who would have knowledge of the work that went into verifying the paintings up for auction."

"You want to tell me why?"

"No, but I think the Chicago Cubs are wonderful."

"You're full of shit," he says, but he gives me a name to call and says I should wait fifteen minutes before I call.

I do, and the man is waiting for my call and eager to help. I've got a feeling Robby is a rather large donor to that museum.

Laurie is in the kitchen, and so when I hang up, I go in and update her on what is going on. "I'll call Corey and Marcus," she says.

Now it's just a matter of waiting for Sam to get back to

me. I think I know what he will say, but I'm still anxious about it.

It's not as bad as waiting for a verdict, but it's nerve-racking.

It's a little past midnight when Sam calls and tells me what I want to hear.

It's all systems go.

Mark Chaikin has been the auctioneer at Echelon for seven years, and has been in the business for almost thirty.

In all that time he has never been involved in a session as important as this one, and never one with nearly as much at stake. One other thing is for sure: there has never been this much public interest before.

Usually these auctions are held among the superelite and interest in them does not penetrate down anywhere near the masses. This time is different; that these pieces were taken and hidden by the Nazis has struck a chord with the public.

Chaikin and Wallace Linder have spent a lot of time going over the mechanics of the event. Even though it is no different from hundreds of other sessions, except in the amount of money, they want to make sure that there are no embarrassing glitches.

There will be a number of people in the audience who will be representing bidders. Those bidders are ultra-wealthy and do not consider it seemly to attend personally and would deem it ultra-embarrassing to be there and lose.

So they will be in cyber contact with their representatives and will be watching the live stream. They can convey bidding instructions to the people on the floor in real time, and those people already know the amounts that they have been authorized to spend.

Linder has announced he will be in the building next door, also owned by Echelon, where their communications center is. He will be fielding electronic bids from those approved buyers who do not have a representative present.

Traditionally, these electronic bids are where the real action is. And since Linder already knows who the huge bidder is going to be, that will certainly be the case here as well.

It's all going to start at 3:00 P.M. . . . just ten minutes from now.

If I am wrong, this is going to be an all-time disaster.

I won't look back on it with regret because Pete Stanton will strangle me, and regrets are hard to have posthumously. Not even the knowledge that my death would cause him and Vince to have to pay for their own food and drink at Charlie's would be enough to make him spare me.

Sam is in a police van watching the auction on live stream and texts me that Wilson Paul is in the audience. That makes me more confident that I am right, but it's still not definite.

Security is stationed at the entrances to both Echelon buildings, the one where the auction is being held, and the communications center next door where Linder is fielding bids.

While the security staff manning the entrances are simply doing their jobs and not involved in anything nefarious, city cops arrive at the scene and quietly take them into custody. If I am right, they can't be allowed to get in the way, even if they are well-intentioned.

In the main room, the pieces are displayed on the stage, each covered in glass. Chaikin painstakingly describes each, an unnecessary exercise because every potential bidder is by now familiar with them.

The net effect of all this is to increase the tension; everyone just wants to get on with the auction.

"The minimum bid, as announced, is one hundred and fifty million dollars," Chaikin says. "Bids will be accepted in twenty-five-million-dollar increments."

He officially opens the bidding with his gavel and there is immediately a bid for the first 150. The bids after that come in rapid succession: 175, 200, 225.

Then a bid for 250 comes from Linder in the communications room. Things have slowed down, but 275 is bid from a representative in the room.

"Do I hear three hundred million dollars?" Chaikin asks, and his buzzer goes off.

He looks at it and appears stunned. It's a bid from the communications room. "I have a bid for five hundred and twenty-five million dollars."

Sam has been updating me on all the bidding, and when he tells me about the huge bid, I turn to Marcus, who has been standing silently next to me, and I give him the okay to kick in the door.

Wallace Linder is sitting at his console, computer open and turned on in front of him.

He is clearly stunned. His door crashing open is not the kind of thing that he would expect to happen; it's probably the first door to be kicked down in Echelon's history.

His cell phone is about three feet from him, and once the initial shock wears off, he makes a move for it. Marcus has already done the same and easily beats him to it.

What Linder doesn't know is that at the same moment Marcus was kicking in the door, the cell towers in the area were being deactivated. Linder's phone number was also rendered inactive by the provider, also at police request. He could not have made a call even by using Wi-Fi.

So the cell phone that Marcus beat him to was actually useless, but there was no sense taking any chances.

"What the hell are you doing?" Linder screams. Then, I suppose thinking I didn't hear him, he repeats more loudly, "What the hell are you doing?"

"There's a long list; I'll try and get through it before the police arrive," I say. "First of all, we're arresting you . . . and Margaret Franklin is being arrested at her home. Second, we're exposing a forgery. Third, we're solving the murder of Stanley Franklin. Fourth, and probably most important, we're preventing a mass tragedy. I think that's everything; I could check my notes."

"You're crazy."

"That's pretty weak, Linder. The auction room is being evacuated right now, and the search for the bomb will turn it up. Your phone is programmed to call the number which would detonate it just by pressing one button."

He just stares at me, so I continue, "I know it doesn't compare to murder and attempted mass murder, but you'll also be charged with art forgery."

"Those paintings are real," he says, but he sounds defeated.

"No, they're not, and I know how you did it. But that's not important now; what's important is that you're going down."

"It was all Margaret," he says softly. I hope my phone recorder is picking it all up. I'm also wearing a wire; which sounds pretty cool to say but is rather uncomfortable.

"No, you pulled the trigger. Bradley was only there to get the gun so that he could include it in the bag dropped near Jeff's house."

"Margaret fired the shots. I was just there to distract him so his back would be turned at the door."

"You two make quite a team."

I text Pete and Laurie to say that everything is good, and moments later police come in through the open door. The only reason they hadn't come in with Marcus and me was in the hope that we could get Linder to further incriminate himself.

Which he did.

Pete Stanton comes in with the first wave of New York cops and stays with me as they take Linder away.

"You are one lucky son of a bitch," Pete says.

"I'm not feeling any gratitude; you'll probably be on the *Today* show in the morning, and it's all because of me."

"But you could have been wrong."

I shrug. "Yeah, there's always a first time for everything." Then, "What's going on now?"

"Take a look out the window."

I do and see that the street is filled with the people who had been at the auction, but police are moving them back to safety. There are also multiple media trucks at the corner. Nobody is going to be allowed to stay too close, in deference to the bomb that we know is in the building.

"The bomb squad is inside?" I ask.

"Yeah, turning the place upside down. They'll find it if it's there. But we might want to get out of here just in case."

"We're safe here. Linder was not about to blow himself up, so the bomb must be in a position where it wouldn't reach where we are."

"Let's leave anyway."

So we do; Marcus comes with us as well. We go out to the street and I see Laurie in the crowd behind the police barricades. Pete gets one of the cops to let her in, and she gives me a large and welcome hug.

"Pete, do I have the smartest and bravest husband in the world?" she asks.

"Not even close," Pete says.

We go to the police van to get Sam, and we all head home. It has probably been the most eventful art auction I've ever attended.

The bomb didn't explode, but the story does.

It isn't often that an attempted mass-murder terrorist attack is foiled on a live stream. And that it happened in New York makes it even bigger news.

Huge money being at stake also contributes to the media obsession . . . so money, power, violence . . . they all combine for something irresistible to the public. The only thing missing for the moment is sex; wait until the world finds out that the two main conspirators, Linder and Margaret Franklin, were having an affair.

Of course, just the media calling it a terrorist attack doesn't make it one; in fact, it misses the point. This was murder for money, with an ingenious forgery plot thrown in.

Pete Stanton is getting a lot of praise for leading the charge, and he's not trying to deflect any of it. So far there's not been much connection to our trial, other than occasional comments that the man who started the conspiracy, Stanley Franklin, was murdered and that someone was recently acquitted of that murder.

I'm sure it won't take long to understand how the trial, murder, forgery, and near bombing are all different pieces of the same puzzle. Then they'll come after me in hordes, but I'll just refer them to Pete.

Actually, I've decided to give one media interview. Since I helped Pete become a media star and a hero in the eyes of the masses, I figured I might as well do something for our other beer-drinking buddy.

So I called Vince and told him I'd give an interview to his reporter Pamela Akers. She is the one who wanted to write a critical story about Stanley Franklin, but had to pass on it when the paper couldn't nail down the details. We're going to do it in our house; she's going to be here any minute.

I call Pete to see if he's learned anything more about what's going on. Since the crimes took place in the city, NYPD has custody of Linder, and Margaret Franklin is there as well.

The New York cops are not into confiding in Pete, but they have told him that Linder is being cooperative and is attempting to throw Margaret Franklin under the legal bus. The evidence against him is overwhelming, as he was caught with a phone programmed to blow up an entire building of people.

Plus the things he said into the wire I was wearing were incriminating by themselves, so Linder is smart enough to know he has no possibility of getting out of this.

Akers comes over and is effusive in her thanks for my granting her the interview. In this media environment, getting this as an exclusive could make her career.

"Vince thanks you also," she says. "He told me to tell you the next beer is on him."

"That would fulfill a dream of mine."

She smiles. "Please try and get a photo of him reaching for his wallet."

She turns on her tape recorder and starts the interview. Laurie comes in to listen because we haven't talked about the details that much, so she wants to learn all about what happened.

I start off by telling Akers that there is much I still don't know, so I will be careful to note when I am telling her fact or educated opinion. I suspect it will all come out as a result of Linder spilling his pretentious guts, but none of that has been made public yet.

She wants to go about this methodically and starts with the explosion at Marstan. Had that not happened, Jeff would never have been charged, and I wouldn't have had to deal with any of this.

"Was the explosion deliberate?"

"Yes," I say. "No question about it. It was done by Tony Bradley, though of course he was being paid to do it."

"Who was paying him?"

"Most likely Stanley Franklin. I'm sure his wife was involved, and I assume Wallace Linder too. Franklin needed the money; his business was failing, so he did it for the insurance.

"By that point I believe the Franklins were involved with Linder in a forgery scheme. They apparently had people overseas that were capable of duplicating these great pieces of art, and they were bringing them into the country through their importing business.

"Stanley Franklin was a true lover of fine art, but he was willing to blow up the pieces because they were fake."

"But why kill all those people?"

"Somehow, through examining the company's financial dealings, they must have stumbled onto what was going on. Maybe they saw that he did not pay big money for the paintings, or to so-called investigators in Europe.

"They were going to confront him with it, so he got rid of them and collected the insurance at the same time."

"So Jeff Wheeler was right."

"About everything. Ironically, the families can now go back and sue the Franklin family and will collect big-time, but Jeff won't be a part of that."

"So he'll get nothing?"

I smile. "Far from it. He'll sue them for conspiring to have him wrongly accused and incarcerated. It's a no-lose case which I will be happy to handle."

"So their big killing . . . if you'll pardon the expression . . . was going to be the auctioning off of these paintings?"

I nod. "Yes."

"How did they fool all the experts?"

"There weren't that many to fool. Remember, the two sets of experts that they claimed signed off on the legitimacy were Franklin's and Echelon's. Obviously that was a setup. The real kicker was getting the Metropolitan Museum people to go along."

"How did they do that? Wasn't radioactive carbon dating done?"

"Yes, on two pieces, but on the canvases, not the painting itself. This is a common practice. But what the forgers did was paint on canvases that dated back to the date of the original paintings. So the canvases matched the dates, therefore the Met people okayed it."

"But they were planning to blow it all up?"

"Yes, again for the insurance money."

"While all the people were there?"

"I believe so, but I can't be sure of that. The important thing was to wait until the bidding was over. Or at least until the huge bid came in."

"Why?"

"A friend of mine said that art is worth what someone is willing to pay for it. That's the crucial point, because the insurance policy did not contain a specific number. It referred to market conditions, meaning that the bidding was the way to determine what it was worth. The higher the bid, the higher the payout from the insurer."

"So there was no high bidder? Linder just made that up?"

"They probably would have credited it to some fictitious Russian oligarch; I can't be sure about that. But no one was going to pay that kind of money; it was a number created for insurance purposes by Linder."

"So your client was just in the wrong place at the wrong time?"

I nod. "Yes. I'm sure that Franklin would have been killed anyway, but when Jeff threatened him in the restaurant, Margaret was there. She realized that Jeff would be the perfect person to blame it on. She got Bradley to plant the evidence."

"I'm still not clear on one thing," Akers says. "Why did they kill Franklin? Wasn't he a part of the conspiracy?"

"I can't say for sure; maybe he got cold feet or was unhappy with the arrangements. But my personal view is that it wasn't about money at all. Margaret Franklin and Wallace Linder were having an affair, and it may just have been a way to get her husband out of the way permanently. It may have been as simple as a love triangle."

I don't tell Akers that I know about the affair because Sam traced Linder's GPS phone records to Margaret's house, and he often spent the night there. I assume that if we were to check Franklin's phone and calendar, we would find out he was out of town on those nights.

Akers has a few follow-up questions, and I tell her I'm available if she thinks of any later on.

Once she leaves, Laurie, who hasn't said a word the entire time, says, "That was damn impressive. You could have given that interview to *Sixty Minutes* and they would have eaten it up."

"But then I would not have the pleasure of drinking a beer paid for by Vince. I'm going to savor every drop."

Our traditional victory party is not at Charlie's this year.

We decided our dogs and especially Rufus should be able to attend, so we're having it at the foundation. Even Sebastian has agreed to honor us with his presence; he walked all the way to the car without having to be lured by a biscuit.

Present, besides the dogs, are Laurie, Ricky, and me; Corey Douglas; Willie Miller and Sondra; Sam Willis; Eddie Dowd; and of course Jeff. Edna couldn't make it; she's exhausted from working on the case.

It's a low-key gathering, we basically just sit and watch our dogs and Rufus play with the dogs up for adoption.

Rufus seems to take a particular liking to a black Lab mix named Boodgey; they wrestle for ten minutes, rest for five, and then it's back to wrestling.

Jeff has some more questions for me about the conspiracy, but since he read my interview in Vince's paper this morning, he's pretty much up-to-date.

Instead we talk about the lawsuit we are going to file against Margaret Franklin and the Stanley Franklin estate. "Will I make enough to pay you your fee?"

I smile. "Many times over."

"I'll never be able to thank you enough. For everything, including giving Rufus such a great home while I was gone."

"He was a model guest. And he loved having siblings."

Jeff nods. "I was thinking about that. Maybe I should get a buddy for him."

"I would encourage it."

He points. "What about that one? Rufus seems to like him. Willie says his name is Boodgey. Can I adopt him?"

I call out, "Hey, Willie. Jeff wants to adopt Boodgey."

Willie smiles broadly; Boodgey is one of his favorites. "I think we can work that out."

"Why don't you do the paperwork. You can take him home tonight. I've got to do something. I'll be back in a half hour or so."

I leave and drive to Charlie's; this is going to be a momentous evening.

Pete and Vince are at our regular table. I think their asses are nailed to the seats. Pete is actually wearing sunglasses, no doubt because of his newly acquired celebrity status.

"That sun is brutal in here," I say.

"Be careful, lawyer," Pete says. "I can turn on you in a second."

"You ready to buy me the beer, Vince? That's why I stopped by."

"You took that seriously?" he says.

"Damn straight. And if you renege, you'll be buying your own beer for the rest of your pathetic life."

That seems to be enough to scare him, and he calls the waiter over. "I want to buy a beer. But I don't want it to be on his tab. I'm paying for it."

The waiter looks skeptical. "You're paying for it?"

"Yes."

The waiter turns to me, disbelieving. "He's paying for it?"

I nod. "Yes, he is."

The waiter nods and starts to leave to get the beer.

"Wait a second," Vince says.

The waiter stops. "Yes?"

"Do I have to buy the whole glassful? Do you sell it by the half glass?"

"No, it's got to be the full glass."

Vince doesn't seem pleased by that. "What if he doesn't finish it? Can I return what he doesn't drink for a refund?"

"This is not Amazon, Vince," I say.

Vince frowns and nods. He says to the waiter, "All right, let's do it." Then he turns to me. "You owe me big-time."

ABOUT THE AUTHOR

Brandy Allen

David Rosenfelt is the Edgar Award–nominated and Shamus Award–winning author of more than thirty Andy Carpenter novels, most recently *Dogged Pursuit*; nine standalone thrillers; two nonfiction titles; and four K Team novels, a series featuring some of the characters from the Andy Carpenter series. After years of living in California, he and his wife moved to Maine with twenty-five of the four thousand dogs they have rescued.